"Stay," he sai~~d~~ **"Stay the night with me. You don't need to go.**

"Upstairs—" Jake murmured, bringing his mouth against hers again, tugging at the jumper and suddenly she froze and shook her head. She couldn't let him remove the jumper. If he removed the jumper then he'd see—

"No—really, we can't."

"Why not? You've already said that there's no one at home to worry about you." His hands were warm on the bare skin of her back and she pulled away quickly. She almost wanted to laugh at the absurdity of the situation. But at the same time she wanted to cry. *Why did he have to come into her life now, when there was absolutely no room for him?*

"I suppose this is the point where I'm supposed to apologize for rushing you." His voice was soft. "But I'm not going to apologize for doing something that feels right."

Dear Reader,

Two years ago I wrote a mountain-rescue trilogy based in the Lake District. I enjoyed the experience so much and received such positive feedback from readers that when my editor invited me to write another seasonal duo, I couldn't resist the temptation to return to the same place.

In the first book, my heroine Christy agrees to spend Christmas with her estranged husband, Alessandro, for the sake of the children even though their marriage is in crisis. Their fiery, passionate relationship has become fractured and weakened through a lack of communication and it seems that nothing can save this particular marriage. But they are given a little outside help in the form of their two children and their best friend, Jake. This book is very special to me because my own children provided much of the inspiration and dialogue.

Having developed a secondary character as delicious as Jake, there was no way I could abandon him without sorting out his life, so the second book is his story. Faced with the prospect of spending yet another Christmas afternoon alone, Jake goes for a walk in the mountains, where he encounters Miranda. She is in the depths of despair and he's just in time to rescue her. But, as it often happens in life, things aren't as they seem and Miranda has secrets. Will Jake be able to accept the person she really is, and will Miranda be able to learn to trust him?

This duo contains a cast of characters who will be familiar to many of my readers, including Sean Nicholson, my very first hero who is still alive in my head and reappears at regular intervals. Fortunately he is aging well and is still as attractive as ever.

I hope you enjoy reading this as much as I enjoyed writing it.

Love,
Sarah

The Midwife's Christmas Miracle

Sarah Morgan

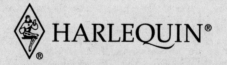

HARLEQUIN®

TORONTO • NEW YORK • LONDON
AMSTERDAM • PARIS • SYDNEY • HAMBURG
STOCKHOLM • ATHENS • TOKYO • MILAN • MADRID
PRAGUE • WARSAW • BUDAPEST • AUCKLAND

ISBN-13: 978-0-373-06579-0
ISBN-10:   0-373-06579-5

THE MIDWIFE'S CHRISTMAS MIRACLE

First North American Publication 2006

This edition published by arrangement with Harlequin Books S.A.

® and TM are trademarks of the publisher. Trademarks indicated with
® are registered in the United States Patent and Trademark Office, the
Canadian Trade Marks Office and in other countries.

www.eHarlequin.com

Printed in U.S.A.

The Midwife's Christmas Miracle

To Julia, for her friendship, brainstorming skills
and staying power.

CHAPTER ONE

SHE'D MADE SUCH A MESS of her life.

Sodden with misery, Miranda sat on the rock, staring at the frozen lake, oblivious to the fact that she was slowly losing the feeling in her fingers and toes.

Around her the mountains rose, wrapped in their lethal covering of snow and ice, but she was as indifferent to their beauty as she was eager for their sanctuary. They offered refuge from glittering tinsel and other symbols of festive cheer.

It was Christmas Day, but up here in the icy wilderness of the Lake District, Christmas Day was just another span of daylight hours without meaning or significance.

And she really shouldn't be crying.

It had been six months. *Six long months.* Time enough to accept the situation and move on. Time enough to forgive herself for being *unforgivably* stupid and naive.

She was supposed to be streetwise. Independent. She was supposed to know everything there was to know about the dark side of human nature. Well, apparently she didn't. She gave a cynical laugh. Apparently even she could be duped.

She'd been stupid and gullible and she just *hated* herself for having been taken in so completely.

With a sniff, she rubbed her numb cheeks with equally

frozen fingers. Crying was pointless and was something she rarely indulged in. Struggling to hold back the tears, Miranda searched inside herself for the fierce strength that she knew she possessed, but all that happened was that more tears welled up in her eyes and spilled down her frozen cheeks. Oh, for goodness' sake! She brushed them away with an impatient hand and wondered what was happening to her. She was *never* usually this pathetic! It was just because it was Christmas. Christmas made everything feel different. At Christmas, everything was focused on the image of the perfect family, but for her to be seduced by that image was completely laughable because she knew better than anyone that families were entirely imperfect.

She didn't want one!

She was better off on her own.

But she'd managed to forget that fact. Briefly, she'd lost all sense of judgment. She, of all people, who had learned long ago that the only person you could truly depend on was yourself. She *never* leaned on people. Never. And yet she'd—

Gritting her teeth, she pushed the thought away. That was in the past now. Whether she liked it or not, it was over and the past didn't matter. All that mattered was the future. And remembering not to make the same mistake again.

She straightened her spine and lifted her chin.

It was time to grow up. That was going to be her New Year's resolution. She was going to stop being such a romantic dreamer and get to grips with the realities of life. Princes didn't ride up on white chargers or horses of any other colour, come to that. Ordinary people didn't win the lottery and families were entirely dysfunctional and not to be envied in the slightest. And Christmas was just one day out of three hundred and sixty-five and it would pass soon enough.

There was absolutely no point in sitting on a rock in the

middle of nowhere, feeling sorry for herself for not having something that just didn't exist.

She needed to pick herself up and make the best of the situation.

Feeling something cold brush her hand, she glanced up and realised with a flash of surprise that it was snowing. Suddenly aware of just how cold she was, she turned her head and noticed with a stab of alarm that she could no longer see the top of the mountains.

The weather had been perfect when she'd left her miserable, cramped, rented flat.

What had happened to the blue sky and the sunshine?

With a flash of panic, she realised that she actually had absolutely no idea where she was. She'd been so desperate to get away from the rows of houses with Christmas trees and fairy-lights—so desperate to escape from the glaring taunt of happy family gatherings—that she'd just climbed onto her rusty, secondhand bike and ridden out of town until the houses had been far behind her and all that had lain ahead had been the mountains. She didn't even know the area because she'd only moved here a week ago.

She'd abandoned the bike in a deserted car park and started to walk, lured by the promise of fresh air, blue sky and the absence of festivities.

Up here on the fells it hadn't seemed like Christmas. Up here, she hadn't felt like the only person on the planet who was surviving Christmas Day on her own. Up here it had just seemed like any other normal day.

Except that her life had reached crisis point.

But the time for reflection had passed and more immediate problems were now pressing in on her. Like finding the car park again. If she were to stand any chance of finding her way down the mountain, she was going to have to leave immediately.

She stood up and stamped the snow off her trainers, realising how totally inadequate they were.

How could she have been so irresponsible?

The answer, of course, was that she hadn't been thinking about anything except her problems, but problems had a way of shifting around and she knew that her immediate problem was one of basic survival.

Trying to identify the way she'd come, she walked for a few minutes and then realised that she could no longer see the ground directly in front of her. She couldn't work out which way was up and which way was down. The path had vanished and beneath her feet lay a lethal, snowy carpet. A treacherous covering that concealed the way home.

The temperature was dropping, she was lost and she had no means of contacting anyone. *No one knew where she was.*

Suddenly understanding the seriousness of her situation, her heart lurched with fear and her mouth dried. Panic gripped her with tight, merciless fingers and for a moment she found it hard to think.

The weather was deteriorating by the minute and she knew absolutely nothing about surviving in freezing, wilderness conditions.

If she walked without knowing where she was going, there was every chance she could walk over a precipice, to her death.

But staying still wasn't an option either. She had no equipment, nothing with which to create warmth or shelter.

Part of her just wanted to sit down and give up. But something stirred inside her. Something that reminded her that giving up wasn't an option. Dying wasn't an option. She *had* to live.

She'd just have to find a way down. Somehow.

She was going to survive.

And once she'd done that, she was going to totally rethink her life.

* * *

Jake Blackwell trudged steadily up the path, noting the change in the weather with a faint smile of amusement. Mountains. A bit like women, he thought to himself as he shifted the pack on his back—unpredictable of mood and always to be treated with respect.

In many ways he preferred unpredictable, wild weather to sunshine and blue skies. Walking and climbing became more of a challenge, a guessing game, a battle of wits between him and the mountain.

The deep snow crunched under his boots, the air was cold enough to numb the face and in the distance he could hear the peal of bells from the village church.

It was Christmas Day.

He should have felt happy.

When he'd set out, the sun had been shining in a perfect blue sky, he'd just enjoyed a traditional turkey dinner with his oldest and dearest friends and watched their children opening presents and playing happily round a twinkling Christmas tree.

The house had been filled with warmth and joy, not least because Alessandro and Christy had finally patched up the holes in their marriage.

He was pleased for them. Relieved. But as he'd closed the door behind him, leaving them to their happiness, a hollow, empty feeling had gnawed at his insides. There was nothing like Christmas to remind you that you were on your own.

It wasn't that he was short of prospective candidates. With a total absence of vanity, he was more than aware that there were no end of midwives and female doctors who were interested in ending his bachelor lifestyle. But none of them interested him. At least, not in the long term.

He dated, of course. He was a healthy, single male so no one expected him to live like a monk. But no matter what happened during the twelve months leading up to Christmas, he always seemed to end the year on his own. No woman had ever held his attention for the long term.

Except Christy, and she'd married his best friend and he'd long since trained himself to put thoughts of her out of his head.

Alessandro was an incredibly lucky guy, he mused. Christy was an amazing woman, the children were beautiful—

With a soft curse he lengthened his stride and talked sense into himself.

What was wrong with being single? Nothing. It was just that it was Christmas Day and all the emphasis seemed to be on families.

That was why he'd chosen to go for a walk instead of returning home to his big, empty house. He could have driven to the hospital and spent the day at work, but why would he want to do that when he'd already spent too much of the year working? In fact, work was probably one of the reasons he was on his own. It was hard to get out and meet people when you were trapped in a hospital day in, day out.

His spirits lifting as he walked, he forced himself to count his blessings. He was healthy, he had a great job at the hospital and he loved his work with the mountain rescue team. He had nothing to complain about.

And if his life sometimes felt a little empty—well, he'd never had trouble filling the void before now.

He walked upwards, enjoying the snow-muffled silence and the cold sting of the air in his lungs.

The visibility was reducing by the moment and he knew he probably ought to turn back. He was familiar with the path and he was well equipped, but he also had a healthy respect for mountains and didn't want to be the one responsible for dragging his colleagues in the mountain rescue team away from their Christmas gatherings.

He was just about to turn back when he caught a flash of colour through the thickening snow. With a quick frown he narrowed his eyes and looked again but it was gone.

It had been so brief that it would have been all too easy to have dismissed the vision as nothing more than a figment of his imagination, but twelve years on the mountain rescue team had honed his instincts and sharpened his brain. So he didn't turn. Instead, he walked forward a few more steps and the stopped dead.

A small figure, half covered in snow, was huddled against a rocky outcrop. A child?

And then the snow-covered figure lifted her head and he saw that it wasn't a child. It was a woman.

And a very beautiful woman.

He couldn't remember ever seeing eyes so exotic. Dark as sloes and framed by thick, lush lashes, they simply accentuated the pallor of her skin. Wisps of damp, ebony hair framed an almost perfect bone structure and the only colour in her face was her mouth—a rich, generous curve of soft pink that might have been designed with the sole purpose of driving a man to distraction.

She looked delicate and feminine and just about the last person he would have expected, or wanted, to find in the mountains in a blizzard.

Snow clung to her hair and her whole body was shivering, and it took just that one glance for him to realise that the situation was serious. This wasn't a seasoned walker, prepared for a hike in the mountains. She looked like a woman who should have been somewhere else entirely.

The shivering was a good sign, he reminded himself grimly as he swung the rucksack off his broad shoulders and delved inside for the equipment he knew he was going to need. When the shivering stopped it meant that the human body was no longer able to produce heat. Still, he didn't need his medical degree or his mountain rescue skills to know that the girl was seriously cold.

He needed to warm her up, check her over and then decide whether he could get her down by himself or whether he was going to need the assistance of his colleagues in the mountain rescue team.

He hoped they'd all enjoyed their Christmas dinner because he had a feeling that he was going to be calling on their services very shortly.

'What are you doing here on your own? Where are your friends?' Dispensing with pleasantries, he selected various items from his rucksack, his movements swift and purposeful as he spoke to the girl, assessing her level of consciousness, knowing that her answers would give clues as to just how cold she was. 'Where are the rest of your party?'

Had the others left her and gone for help? Didn't they have the sense to know that someone should have stayed with her? Or were they in trouble, too?

For a long moment she didn't answer him and he wondered with a flash of concern whether she was too cold to speak. Had his first judgment of the situation been wrong?

'What's your name?' His tone was urgent now and he crouched down to her level and took her face in his hands, forcing her to look at him. 'Tell me your name.'

Speak to me. Say something.

Drowsiness and confusion were signs of the onset of hypothermia and he didn't like what he was seeing.

Her dark eyes slid to his and he saw something in her gaze that twisted his insides. An empty hopelessness.

'Miranda.' Finally she spoke and her voice seemed tiny in the huge emptiness of snow and ice. 'No friends. No party.' Her arms were huddled round her waist for warmth. 'Just m-me.'

'Here, sit on this.' Jake pushed a thick pad underneath her, reminding himself that there would be time enough later to talk to her about the dangers of walking alone in winter weather conditions. 'It's insulated and it will stop the snow seeping through your clothes. Then we need to get you something to eat.'

Mentally he ran through the various stages of hypothermia.

He knew that the most effective warming of the casualty came from the inside. She needed glucose and fluid and he needed to stop her losing any more heat.

He handed her a chocolate bar and then pulled a fleece hat onto her damp hair to try and prevent further heat loss from her head.

The chocolate bar slipped through her fingers and her eyes drifted closed. 'Not really hungry. Tired now…' she murmured, and he cursed softly under his breath as he rescued the chocolate.

'You need to eat, Miranda. It will warm you up.' He pulled the wrapper off the chocolate, pushed the bar into her hands again and closed her fingers around it. 'Eat!'

Her eyes opened at his sharp command and she stared blankly at the chocolate bar as if she'd never seen one before and then took a reluctant nibble.

Jake removed her sodden coat, which would have struggled to give protection against a light shower in the city, let alone heavy snow in the mountains.

'Don't take my coat off.' She mumbled her protest and tried to stop him but he'd already dropped it on the ground and was dragging extra layers from his rucksack.

'You need to put these on. You need dry clothes. Put on this fleece and then this waterproof shell.'

She stared at the clothes he dropped onto her lap and he gave a sigh and picked them up, deciding that he was going to have to dress her himself. So he pulled the fleece over her head and then manoeuvred her arms through the sleeves, then did the same thing again with another layer and finally zipped her into his spare coat.

It was like dressing a doll. She was limp and unresisting and his coat swamped her, but at least it was dry and weatherproof. He wrapped a scarf around her mouth and nose to warm the air she was breathing, running through the options in his head. Helicopter evacuation? Not in this weather. Which meant calling the team out. But it would take them a couple of hours to reach this point and that was two hours during which Miranda could grow even colder.

'All right.' Pleased to see that she'd finished the chocolate bar, he handed her another and reached into his rucksack for the insulated flask that he always carried. 'This is the situation. We basically have two choices. I can contact the mountain rescue team and then put up a shelter and we can lie naked in a sleeping bag together while we wait. That should warm you up.'

Her eyes slid to his and he saw a glimmer of humour. 'Is that an indecent proposal?'

Something in her slightly cynical tone made him smile. She had a sense of humour and that was a good sign. 'Believe it or not, it wasn't. Skin to skin contact is the fastest way of re-warming a casualty.'

Her teeth were chattering as she nibbled reluctantly on the second chocolate bar. 'That's the most original seduction line I've ever heard and, believe me, I've heard a few.' Her voice was weak and rasping. 'And I'm not a casualty.'

He decided not to point out that she was fast becoming one. 'The second choice is that we walk down. But that requires you to get up and move your legs. Are you up to it?'

'Of course.' More alert now, she rubbed the snow out of

her eyes with the back of her hand. 'What do you think I am? Pathetic?'

No, hypothermic.

He was relieved to see that she suddenly seemed to be waking up. 'So tell me what you're doing out here on a day like this.' Concern made his voice sharper than he'd intended. 'Do you have a death wish?'

'No. And the day was nothing like this earlier this morning. It was sunny.' Despite the extra layers he'd given her, her teeth were still chattering and her breath clouded the freezing air. 'And I was out for a walk, just like you.'

Jake glanced down at her feet and lifted an eyebrow. '*Not* like me,' he pointed out gently. 'You're wearing trainers.'

Her hands still clutching the chocolate bar, the girl stared down at her feet and gave a wan smile. 'Well, they were all I had. I don't possess walking boots. I thought I'd be all right providing I stuck to the path.'

'Is this the same path that has just disappeared under a layer of snow? And didn't you possess gloves either?' Jake gave a sigh and reached inside his rucksack again. 'If you don't own walking boots then you shouldn't be out on the mountains, especially not at the height of winter. What were you thinking of?'

For a moment those incredible eyes were haunted by ghosts and then she turned her head away. 'Oh, I don't know,' she said huskily. 'This and that. Stuff.'

Stuff?

Something about the set of her profile made him frown and want to question her further but then he reminded himself that hesitation could make the difference between life and death in the mountains. This wasn't the time for polite conversation. 'Finish the chocolate.' He laid a pair of gloves on her lap. 'And then put these on before you develop frostbite in your fingers. Have you any idea what the temperature is today?'

She finished the last of the chocolate and then slowly wriggled her hands into the gloves. 'No, but it certainly isn't the Bahamas, that's for sure. The sun was shining when I left.'

It was a common mistake, Jake reflected. Believing that a cloudless blue sky would last. A significant proportion of the calls to the mountain rescue team were made by people who had underestimated the changeability of the weather. 'You shouldn't be out here on your own in this weather. It's Christmas Day, you should be home with family, eating turkey.' The moment the words left his mouth he wanted to kick himself. Presumably, if that had been an option she would have taken it, and her next words confirmed his suspicion.

'I don't have any family.' She spoke the words calmly, as if it wasn't that great a problem. 'But you're completely right, of course. Coming out here was a stupid thing to do. It's just that it was beautiful and I needed to think and—'

'And you didn't want to sit in by yourself on Christmas Day. You don't have to explain to me.' He gave a wry smile. 'All around the country at this precise moment in time, people are opening presents they don't want from relatives they haven't seen all year and gaining pounds that they're going to spend the next few months failing to lose.'

'So is that what you're doing up here in the wilderness? Avoiding presents and weight gain?' Her gaze rested on his shoulders and then lifted to his mouth and lingered there for a moment. Then she lifted her eyes to his again and he felt something stir inside him. The urge to kiss her was so powerful that he forced himself to take a step backwards, reminding himself that this wasn't the time or the place.

Or the woman. He didn't know what her problem was, but it was clearly something significant.

'I happen to love it up here in the wilderness.' He watched as she slowly stood up. 'It's my favourite place.'

'Oh.' She hugged her arms around her body to try and stop the shivering. 'Well, lucky for me that you happened to be passing. If you'll just point me in the right direction, I'll make my way home. Sorry to have bothered you and eaten all your chocolate rations. I hope there are plenty more waiting for you back on your Christmas tree.'

He was torn between exasperation and admiration. He knew she was hideously cold and uncomfortable. Every other female he knew would have been moaning, hysterical or both by now. Miranda seemed remarkably calm. *Too calm?*

'This isn't a shopping centre with a hidden exit. Do you have any idea how much danger you're in?'

'Yes, actually,' she said calmly, stamping her feet to clear her trainers of the snow. 'But I assume that panicking isn't going to help. Better to make a plan and get on with it.'

'And that's what you were doing, sitting on the rock, when I found you? Planning?'

'Actually, I was trying to work out which way was up and which way was down.' She squinted through the steady fall of snow. 'I didn't want to move until I was sure and everything seems to have merged. You can't tell the difference between the sky and the ground.'

Jake gave a disbelieving shake of his head. 'It's called a whiteout,' he informed her gently, wondering what would have happened to her if he hadn't chosen to take this particular path. 'One of the most dangerous weather conditions that exists in the mountains.'

'I've never seen one before.' She stretched out a hand and caught some of the thick snowflakes as they landed. 'Gosh.'

'Gosh? *Gosh?*' Shaking his head with exasperation, Jake lifted the flask. 'Here—drink some of this.' He poured the creamy liquid into the cup and handed it to her.

'What is it? I don't drink alcohol.'

'And I don't give alcohol to victims of hypothermia. It would kill them.'

She lifted her chin and her dark eyes flashed with anger. 'I'm *not* a victim.' Her tone was chilly. 'Don't ever call me a victim.'

He found himself wondering why that one word seemed to trouble her more than her immediate situation. 'You will be a victim if we don't warm you up soon. It's hot chocolate. It will give you energy and warm you up.' He pushed the flask into her gloved hands. 'Stop talking and drink.'

'Hot chocolate? You keep pulling amazing things out of your bag.' Her teeth were chattering again as she clutched the mug. 'Clothes and now hot drinks. Who are you, Father Christmas?'

'A well-equipped climber,' he said pointedly, and she stared into the mug without enthusiasm.

'We can't all afford fancy equipment.'

'It isn't about fancy equipment! It's about safety. And if you don't have the right equipment, you shouldn't be out here.' He heard his voice sharpen and stopped talking. What was the matter with him? He never lectured people. On the contrary, he believed that people had the right to live their lives the way they wanted to live them. But he didn't feel remotely relaxed about Miranda.

What if she did the same thing again and he wasn't around to rescue her?

He shook himself, wondering why he cared so much about someone he'd known for less than an hour.

She sipped the chocolate. 'Oh...' She closed her eyes and gave a low moan of delight. 'That's delicious. I've never tasted anything better in my life.'

Looking at the thickness of her dark lashes and the vulnerability of her soft mouth, Jake felt a thud of lust and almost laughed at himself.

He really needed to get out more. His life was truly in a sorry state if he was lusting after a half-frozen woman whose knowledge of the mountains could have been written on a bootlace.

She drank the chocolate and he pushed the Thermos back into his rucksack and withdrew a rope and harness.

'I'm going to put this on you because your footwear has no grip and the ground is slippery.'

She looked at the rope. 'You're going to lower me down the mountain?'

'We're going to *walk* down the mountain. I'm going to tie you to me,' he explained patiently. 'That way, if you slip, I catch you.'

'Or I pull you over, too.'

He refrained from pointing out that he had more muscle in one arm than she appeared to have in her entire body. 'That isn't going to happen.'

She took a deep breath and gave him a slightly chilly smile. 'Thanks for the chocolate and the extra layers. I'll be fine now. I can get down by myself. If you give me your address, I'll deliver your things back to you after Christmas.'

He stared at her, unable to believe what he was hearing. 'You'll be fine?'

By rights she should be clinging to him, begging him not to leave her. Instead, she was dismissing him.

'Absolutely fine.' Her eyes were filled with determination. 'I'm warm again now so I don't need any more help, although I'd love to borrow the hat. I'm sorry to have bothered you this much.'

'Bothered me?' He frowned at her, wondering what was going through her head. 'Miranda, you don't have a clue where you are and you don't have any equipment to help you survive in these weather conditions. Just how, precisely, do you plan to get yourself down on your own?'

'If you'd be kind enough to just point me towards the path and tell me when I go left or right, I'll be fine.'

He blinked. She sounded like someone asking for directions in a city. 'The path,' he pointed out gently, 'is currently buried under several centimetres of snow. And it doesn't go left or right—it curves, subtly. Step too far to the left and you'll find yourself at the bottom of the valley faster than you'd planned, step too far to the right and you'll fall into the ravine.'

Her smile faltered slightly. 'I'm sure I'll manage.'

He struggled to keep the sarcasm out of his voice. 'How?'

'Because I'm used to doing things by myself. I'm a survivor,' she said firmly, and there was something in her tone that made Jake look at her searchingly.

Was she trying to convince him or herself?

As intrigued as he was puzzled, he gave a quick shake of his head. One minute she was chatty and then next distracted, far away, as if she had something more important on her mind than survival.

What was the matter with her?

And what was she doing up here on her own on Christmas Day?

Ignoring her attempts to dismiss him, he fastened the rope to the harness on her waist with swift, skilled movements of his hands. 'Do you even know which way is down?'

'No. But it sounds as if I'm going to find it soon enough if I take a wrong step.'

'You're not going to take a wrong step.' He checked the knot on the rope.

'I don't want you to give up your walk to rescue me.'

She was clearly fiercely independent. He rubbed a hand across his face to clear his vision and tried another tack. 'I'd already finished my walk so we're walking in the same direction anyway.'

'Oh. Well, that's different. If you're going that way…' she shrugged '…we might as well walk together. Why do you have all this equipment?'

'Part of my job.'

'Your job?'

Jake gave the rope a gentle tug. He'd decided to keep the rope short so that if she slipped it would reduce the sliding distance. 'I'm in the mountain rescue team. And if we don't both go down now, we'll be calling out the entire team later, which would be extremely embarrassing for me.'

She stared dubiously at the mist and snow. 'All right. I suppose it makes sense to walk together. I can certainly see why they call it a whiteout.'

'Can you walk?'

'Of course.' She looked affronted and stamped her feet as if to prove that they were still working. 'I'm just cold.'

'It's just that most people walking in trainers in this weather end up with a sprained ankle at the very least,' he drawled, securing the top of his rucksack and swinging it back onto his back. 'But if you're intact, we'll get going.'

'How far is it?'

'Don't you know?'

She shook her head. 'I didn't really notice the time. I just walked…'

Something in her voice made him take a closer look at her. *Why* had she just walked? What had occupied her mind so totally that she hadn't noticed the time or the change in the weather?

Telling himself that it was none of his business, Jake checked the rope one more time and then jerked his head in the direction of the path. 'Come on. This way.'

She squinted forward. 'It all looks the same to me. How do you know where the path is supposed to be?'

'Because I know this walk well and I recognise the terrain.'

He walked steadily, matching his pace to hers and keeping a close eye on her.

She was cold, he could see that, but nowhere near as cold as she'd been when he'd found her. They weren't far from the car park now so he wasn't too worried.

He was more worried about the blank, slightly vacant look in her huge dark eyes. Once they started to walk she sank into silence, her eyes straight ahead, stepping where he told her to step.

He sensed that something was very wrong.

Was it was just the pressures of Christmas Day? Was she avoiding everyone else's happiness?

They reached the car park without mishap and he reached down and detached the rope from her waist.

'We're here.' He glanced around him with a frown. At this level, the mist had lifted sufficiently to improve the visibility but he could only see one car. His. 'Where did you park?'

'Oh.' She blinked and took a deep breath as if waking herself up. 'Over there.'

His gaze followed the direction of her vague gesture but he saw nothing. 'Your car's been stolen.'

It happened, of course, in these isolated car parks.

'No.' She shook her head and gave him a wan smile as she handed back the harness. 'I don't have a car. I have a bike.'

A bike? He stared again and finally saw a rusty, ancient bicycle propped against a tree.

'That's yours?'

'Yes.' She pulled the hat from her head and he frowned.

'What are you doing?'

'Returning your clothes. Thank you so much.'

'Stop. Wait…' He put the hat back on her head, feeling her silky hair brush his fingers. 'You can't get on that bike and cycle—you're frozen.' And he didn't want her to leave. He wanted to get to know her. *He wanted to—*

'I'll warm up when I get back to my—' She broke off and flinched slightly. 'Home. I'll be fine at home.'

Was he imagining things or had her voice changed when she'd said the word 'home'? He was picking up all sorts of signals but so far he wasn't sure what any of them meant.

But he intended to find out.

'What are your plans now? Are you spending the rest of the day with friends?'

She stared at him for a long time and then shook her head slowly. 'No,' she said quietly, 'I'm not. But I'll be fine. I always am.'

Why was someone like her spending the day on her own?

Suddenly he had an urgent desire to know what was wrong—what had brought that haunted look to her face. *And he had an even more urgent desire to drag her into his arms and kiss her until her pale cheeks gained some colour.*

Unable to remember a time when he'd had such a powerful reaction to a woman, Jake closed his hand over her wrist, unwilling to let her go.

'Come on.' Without questioning the impulse, he strode purposefully over to his car with her in tow. Still with one hand around her slender wrist, he opened his boot, slung his gear inside and then opened the passenger door. 'Hop in. I'll get your bike.'

'What do you mean, hop in?' She stared at the car and then at him and he gave a shrug and his most non-threatening smile.

'It's Christmas Day, Miranda, and you and I seem to be the only two people on the planet that don't have someone to spend it with. So I suggest we spend it together. You can warm up at my place and we can sprawl on my sofas and watch endless movies.'

And get to know each other.

Her gaze became as cold as the weather and she tried to pull away from him. 'No, thank you.'

'It wasn't an indecent proposal,' he drawled softly, releasing her immediately. 'Just a friendly one. No hidden agenda.'

Her slender body was tense. Poised. 'Everyone has a hidden agenda.'

'All right—you caught me.' He leaned against his car and smiled. 'I do have a hidden agenda and it's entirely selfish. I don't want to be on my own on Christmas Day. I get morose. That's why I was in the mountains. I saved you so now you need to save me. Keep me company.'

Her eyes met his. And then she looked away and gave a tiny shake of her head, as if she was feeling something that she didn't want to feel. 'This is ridiculous. I don't—'

Suddenly it seemed imperative that he persuade her. *He wasn't going to let her go.* 'Do you have anywhere else you have to be?'

'No.' Her dark eyes clouded and she looked away from him, staring into the distance with a slightly blank expression on her beautiful face. 'I don't.'

'So what's the problem?'

Her eyes lifted to his again, her gaze solemn and considering. 'All right. Just for a few hours.'

Wondering why her answer had lifted his spirits so much, Jake bundled her inside the car and retrieved her bike.

Suddenly he was looking forward to the rest of Christmas Day.

CHAPTER TWO

MIRANDA lay in the hot bath with her eyes closed, feeling the delicious warmth spread back through her frozen limbs.

On the chair at the far side of the huge bathroom lay the neat pile of clothes that the man had given her.

The man...

The knowledge that she hadn't, so far, even asked his name brought a faint smile of derision to her face.

She should probably be worried, but she wasn't.

Strangers didn't frighten her. She knew from experience that hurt and pain most often came from those who were familiar and close to you, not from strangers. When there was a murder, didn't the police start by questioning the family?

No, she wasn't afraid of strangers and she certainly wasn't afraid of the man who had rescued her.

And now, right at this precise moment, she was glad of her impulsive decision to accept his invitation.

It was Christmas Day. *And she hated Christmas Day.* There was no reason at all why she had to hurry back to her miserable, lonely flat.

It was important that she looked after herself.

And it was just for one day.

After that, she'd vanish into the sunset and never see him

again. And she had no reason to feel guilty about that because he had been the one who'd insisted that she spend the rest of the day with him because he hated Christmas, too.

She frowned and slid deeper under the water. Why would a man like him hate Christmas Day? She would have thought that women would have been lining up at his door, fighting over who was going to help him hang baubles on his tree.

But she knew better than anyone that life didn't always send you what you deserved. Which was why it was important to make the most of the moment and that was exactly what she was doing right now.

Having justified her actions to herself, she allowed herself to just enjoy the delicious sensation of warmth and hummed softly, luxuriating in the hot, scented water until she felt her eyelids droop. With a determined effort she forced them open again.

Not very sensible to be rescued from a freezing mountain, only to drown in a steaming bath, she thought as she turned off the tap and lifted herself reluctantly from the water. It was the only way to ensure that she stayed awake.

Aware that her rescuer would probably come looking for her if she didn't reappear soon, she reluctantly stood up and reached for the towel he'd left out for her. It was wonderful to feel warm after being so very, very cold. Vowing to buy some books on safety in the mountains before venturing out again, she dried herself and then examined the pile of clothes he'd given her.

She pulled on a pair of fleecy tracksuit bottoms and the jumper and then sat down on the chair and started to laugh. She looked completely ridiculous. If she'd needed a reminder of the differences between their physiques then she had it now. The trousers were at least a foot too long and the sleeves of the jumper hung several inches past the tips of her fingers.

The clothes acted as a wake-up call.

What on earth was she doing here?

She was behaving like Goldilocks, wandering lost in a forest and seeking shelter.

Why exactly had she decided to accept his invitation? She'd been all ready to refuse but there was something about him that had made it impossible to say no.

He'd rescued her when she'd been lost and, in a way, part of her was still lost.

Wiping the steam from the bathroom mirror, she stared at her reflection for a moment. She looked more like Snow White than Goldilocks, with her pale skin and the black rings under her eyes. She wasn't sleeping well and she knew that she had to do something about it. She needed to rest. She needed to think about—

'Miranda?'

The sound of a deep male voice from the other side of the door made her jump and she turned with a start. 'Yes?'

'Are you decent?'

'Oh, yes, I—'

The door opened and he strolled into the room. Her heart missed a beat. He was a man who would always attract the attention of women, and not just because of the athletic power of his physique. He'd changed into a pair of snug-fitting black jeans and a blue jumper almost the exact colour of his eyes. His damp hair suggested that there was obviously another bathroom somewhere in his house.

His gaze lingered on hers for several long seconds and she felt warmth seep into her cheeks. Suddenly her heart pumped harder and a dangerous, liquid heat uncurled deep inside her. Something happened when she looked at him. Something that she'd never felt before.

Then he ran a hand over the back of his neck and his gaze turned from searching to amused. 'Not exactly the same size, are we?'

Her heart still pumping, she pushed the sleeves of his jumper up her arms in an attempt to find her hands. 'They're great. Perfect.'

They covered everything, which was what she wanted.

She wasn't in the mood to offer explanations.

'Turn the legs up or you'll break your neck on my stairs,' he advised, reaching for a dry towel from the pile and handing it to her. 'Come on. There's a fire in the living room. It's really cosy. You can dry your hair in there.'

She rolled up the legs of the trousers and followed him, unable to resist the temptation to peep as she walked along the landing and down the stairs.

His house was huge, she thought wistfully. Huge and gorgeous. Polished wood floors, soft rugs and huge windows, it succeeded in being stylish and welcoming at the same time.

He intercepted her glance. 'My sister's an interior designer. She can't resist the temptation to manage my living space. It's called interfering.'

'Lucky you.' What wouldn't she have given to have a sibling to interfere in her life?

Pushing away the thought, she followed him into the large living room. More huge windows overlooked the garden and the lawn sloped down to the shore of the lake. The mist had lifted, the snow had stopped and in the distance the fells rose, snowy and breathtakingly beautiful.

A crackling log fire formed the focus of the room and Miranda found herself wanting to sink down onto the thick, opulent rug and purr like a cat.

It was hard to believe that people actually lived like this, she mused as she looked at the exquisite painting above the fire. It all seemed a million miles from her real life.

Then her eyes rested on a photograph on the mantel-piece. There was no mistaking the man in the photo. The same wicked blue eyes, the same cropped dark hair and dangerous smile. And he was rolling in the snow with two laughing children.

She picked it up, the warmth draining from her body, her mouth so dry she could hardly form the words. 'Are they yours? Are you married?' She almost laughed at herself. Of course he was married! Why would a man like him be single?

'They're my nephews—my sister's children. I'm not married.' His eyes narrowed and his gaze was suddenly intent. 'Do you think I'd have invited you back here if I was married with children? Do I look as though I'm married?'

'Appearances can be deceptive.' Hoping that he didn't notice that her hand was shaking, she put the photograph carefully back on the table.

This was ridiculous.

She ought to leave, she thought to herself, suddenly unsettled by the feelings she was having.

But then she thought of the small, freezing bedroom with the bare walls and peeling paintwork that awaited her. She was in no hurry to go home.

If he wasn't married, what harm could it do to stay? She wasn't hurting anyone.

Just for the rest of the day, she promised herself, and then she'd go back to the harsh reality of her life.

She sank down onto the sofa. It was deep and squashy and comfortable and suddenly she just wanted to curl up and sleep. 'This is a lovely room.'

'Thanks. What can I get you to drink?' He stood by the fire, fingers hooked into the pockets of his jeans as he watched her. 'Wine? Champagne?'

'Oh.' She brushed her damp hair away from her face. 'Something non-alcoholic, please. Juice? Tonic?'

'It's Christmas. Don't you fancy anything stronger?'

'No, thanks. I have to cycle home later. I don't want to be drunk in charge of a heap of rust.'

He smiled and handed her a glass. 'So where's home, Miranda? And why were you avoiding Christmas Day?'

'It's just not my favourite time,' she said evasively, and he gave a wry smile of understanding.

'Too much of the media portrayal of happy families?'

'Oh, no. That's all nonsense.'

His blue eyes lingered on hers. 'Is it?'

'Of course.' She curled her legs under her and grinned at him. 'It's an image created by advertisers would have you believe that the perfect family exists, but it doesn't. At least, only on the surface. Underneath, it's all very different.'

'Different in what way?'

'Things are never as they appear on the surface. All families have secrets.' She sipped at her drink. 'Take the family in that yoghurt advert on television.'

He smiled. 'I know the one you mean. Healthy, happy and smiling. Two children and a dog. The sun is shining and there isn't a cloud in the sky.'

'That's the one.' She put her drink down on the small table next to the sofa, laughter in her eyes. 'But do you want to know the truth? The father is probably having an affair with his wife's best friend and the wife doesn't know yet but wouldn't care anyway because she has a secret life as a high-class escort whenever her husband is away on business. It actually suits her that he isn't around much because she doesn't particularly enjoy his company except when they're eating yoghurt in front of a film crew.'

Amusement flickered in his gaze and he tilted his head to one side as he listened. 'And the children?'

She nestled more deeply in the sofa, wondering why he was so easy to talk to. 'The girl has been so damaged by the lack of attention from her parents that she's now shoplifting regularly with her friends and has already started smoking and taking drugs behind the toilets at school, and the little boy is being badly bullied but hasn't told anyone and no one has noticed because they don't show enough interest in each other as individuals.' She stopped and took a breath and he lifted a dark eyebrow in question. The amusement in his eyes had been replaced by speculation.

'And the dog? Looked like a perfectly good-natured Labrador to me. No vices. Are you about to tell me that he's bitten the neighbour and needs a doggy psychiatrist?'

She laughed. 'They've received an official warning from the police because he regularly fouls the pavement and barks so loudly that he wakes the neighbours. So far he hasn't actually bitten anyone but don't think that just because he looks friendly he can't have a bad side. Dogs and people have a way of surprising you.'

'That's right. They do.' He studied her closely. 'Sounds like the family from hell.'

Her smile faded. 'A pretty normal family, actually. I'm just making the point that the picture presented by the media falls short of the real thing. Families are full of imperfections.'

'Is that your experience?'

She realised suddenly that she'd said too much. *Revealed more than she'd intended.* 'It's the truth.'

He swirled the last of his drink around his glass. 'I agree that families are complicated,' he said slowly, 'and I agree that it's pretty hard to find the right person and make it all work in today's fast-paced, driven, consumer-orientated environment. And I think happiness is probably something different for each person. The important thing is to find someone like-minded and then live your own definition of happiness together.'

She stared at him. 'You really believe that?'

'Why wouldn't I?'

'Because it's a romantic view of relationships.'

'I disagree. I think it's a realistic view.'

'Believing that a family can be truly happy isn't realistic.'

His gaze was searching. 'Clearly you've never met anyone in a good relationship.'

'Neither have you.' She lifted her drink. 'You can't judge a family by watching from the outside. You have to be on the inside to know the truth. You probably have friends who you *think* are happy…'

A slight frown touched his brows and something flickered across his face. 'I have friends who I *know* are happy,' he said softly, and she shook her head.

'*How* do you know? Are you there when the door closes and they're left alone together? Do you know anything about the rows that they have in private?'

'No, but I know a lot about the rows they have in public,' he said dryly, reaching for the bottle and topping up his drink. 'He's Spanish and she's Irish and to call their relationship volatile would probably be to risk accusations of understatement but, believe me, they're happy. It might not work for everyone, but it works for them. And that's what I mean when I say you have to find someone who wants what you want. One person's happy marriage is another person's living hell.'

Miranda felt the cold trickle down her spine. *She knew everything there was to know about hell.*

For a moment she sat in frozen silence and then felt the sofa dip as he sat down next to her.

'Tell me about yourself. Tell me what you're thinking about.'

She shook the shadows away from her mind. 'Nothing.' She'd already said far too much. She smiled at him and handed him her empty glass. 'So—given that you're such a romantic, why aren't you married?'

He pulled a face. 'I'm not sure that I'm particularly romantic. And I don't have a wife because I happen to be picky about who I spend the rest of my life with.' The gleam in his blue eyes made her heart skip and dance and she gave herself a sharp talking-to. It wasn't so long ago she'd fallen for a charming smile and smooth patter. She wasn't about to do it again in a hurry.

He put her empty glass down on the table. 'If you ask me, the biggest problem with relationships is the reality gap.'

'Reality gap?'

'The gap between reality and expectations. People are basically flawed. If you expect families to be perfect then you're doomed to disappointment.'

'Maybe.' She was suddenly very aware of him. 'Do you realise that I haven't even asked your name?'

He smiled. 'It's Jake. Jake Blackwell.'

She nodded. The name fitted the man, she decided, leaning her head back against the sofa. Strong. Masculine. 'Well, Jake Blackwell, I haven't thanked you properly for rescuing me today.'

'It was my pleasure.' His gaze lingered on her face. 'It's good to have company on Christmas Day. But promise me you won't go out in the mountains again without the proper equipment and experienced company.'

She lifted her head. 'I'll do something about the equipment but the company is outside my control. I've only just moved to the area. I don't know anyone.'

'You know me.' His quiet statement hovered in the air between them and there was something in his eyes that made her stomach flip.

She gave herself a mental shake and looked away, determined to ignore all the signals that her body was sending her. Mind over matter. Common sense over chemistry.

'I'm sure you have better things to do than walk with a complete beginner who thinks that a whiteout is something you can achieve with a good washing powder.'

He laughed. 'Not really. Any time you want to walk in the hills, I'll be happy to act as escort.'

'Thank you.' Her voice was husky and she still didn't dare meet his eyes. Neither did she think it worth telling him that, after today, she wouldn't be seeing him again.

How could she?

It just wasn't possible. Her life was already more complicated than she would ever have believed possible and so far she hadn't begun to work out how she was going to unravel it all. And, anyway, he probably wasn't interested in tomorrow either. Hadn't he been honest about the fact that he just didn't want to spend Christmas Day on his own?

'You ought to eat something. I'll go and raid the kitchen and then we can sprawl on the sofa and watch agonisingly awful Christmas television. We can spend the afternoon guessing what's really happening behind the happy families.'

'Sounds good to me.'

He brought out a selection of food and switched on the television but, in the end, they talked more than they watched and it was dark by the time Miranda glanced at her watch and realised how late it was.

She really ought to be going, she thought reluctantly, but somehow couldn't find the enthusiasm or motivation necessary to move. And was that surprising? All that awaited her was a cold, cheerless bedroom in an equally cheerless flat. But at least it was cheap, which was the important thing. At the moment she just needed to save her money.

Jake had retreated to the kitchen in search of more food and she flicked idly through the channels, stopping at the picture of a sad-looking child. The narrator informed her in low, mournful tones that the little girl was just one of many children waiting for adoption who would be without parents this year.

Miranda felt tears prick her eyes and blinked furiously. What on earth was the matter with her? Then she gave a sigh. She knew *exactly* why she was feeling so emotional, but it didn't make it any easier to cope with!

Strolling back into the room with a plate full of warm mince pies, Jake deposited them on the nearest table and sat down next to her on the sofa. 'You look really sad. What's the matter? Are you crying?'

Horrified at her uncharacteristic lack of control, she summoned up a smile, wishing he hadn't chosen that precise moment to come back into the room. 'Of course I'm not crying. Just a bit tired, I think.' It was a partial truth. 'Just ignore me. I need to go home and go to bed.'

'Not until you've sampled these gorgeous mince pies. And if you think I'm going to let you go home when you're upset, you don't know me. It's still early. There's no hurry.' His expression was concerned. 'I wish you'd tell me what's the matter. Is it the whole Christmas thing?'

'No. I'm just being stupid.' Despite her best efforts, her eyes filled again. She heard him give a soft curse and then she was pulled into his arms.

He was all hard muscle and masculine strength and for a long, indulgent moment she closed her eyes and allowed herself the luxury of leaning on someone. *Just for a moment,* she promised herself. What harm could it do?

Then he released her slightly and slipped his fingers under her chin, tilting her face to look at him. 'You're very beautiful, do you know that?' His voice was low and husky and she felt her heart bang hard against her ribs as she stared into those, blue, blue eyes.

Pull away now, Miranda, a voice said inside her head, but she suddenly found that she couldn't move.

His gaze lingered on hers, dropped to her mouth and then his head lowered.

And he kissed her. Gently at first, his mouth brushing over hers, his gaze holding her trapped. Then he coaxed her lips apart with the tip of his tongue and slid both hands into her hair, holding her head steady while he took the kiss several stages further.

Her eyes drifted shut and suddenly she felt as though she were falling. Her head spun, her body felt suddenly weak and everything inside her was either pounding or fluttering.

Never before, in her entire adult life, had she felt like this.

By the time he finally lifted his head, she couldn't remember why she'd been crying. She couldn't remember anything.

'Oh… You… I should go,' she muttered in a feeble attempt to regain some sort of control.

'Stay,' he breathed, his mouth inches from hers. 'Stay the night with me and we'll spend tomorrow together. You don't need to go.'

Her senses shimmered with awareness and everything weakened. She didn't want to feel it. She didn't want to feel anything. Feeling meant vulnerability and vulnerability just meant pain. 'Work tomorrow. I have to go…home…' She stumbled over the word because no one in their right mind could really apply that word to a grotty room with damp patches on the walls and a threadbare carpet.

'Tomorrow,' he groaned, bringing his mouth against hers again. 'You can go home tomorrow.'

How had he ever learned to kiss like that? she wondered dreamily as his mouth transported her to a different place entirely. Threadbare carpets and cranky landlords were forgotten as she was enveloped in a sensual cloak of erotic anticipation. Suddenly everything seemed perfect, even though things were about as far from perfect as they could get.

'Upstairs…' Jake murmured, tugging at the jumper, and she suddenly froze and shook her head. She couldn't let him remove the jumper. If he removed the jumper then he'd see—

'No—really, we can't.'

'Why not? You've already said that there's no one at home to worry about you.' His hands were warm on the bare skin of her back and she pulled away quickly.

She almost wanted to laugh at the absurdity of the situation. But at the same time she wanted to cry. *Why did he have to come into her life now, when there was absolutely no room for him?*

'I suppose this is the point where I'm supposed to apologise for rushing you.' His voice was soft. 'But I'm not going to apologise for doing something that felt completely right.'

She bit her lip and waited for the frantic bump of her heart to slow to something approaching normal levels. 'Did I see you bring a mince pie into the room?'

His mouth was still close to hers. 'Are you changing the subject?'

'Yes.' She wished he wouldn't look at her like that. There was a sexy gleam in those wicked blue eyes that made it almost impossible to concentrate. 'I'm hungry.'

He hesitated briefly and then sat back. 'You have a ferocious appetite for a woman,' he drawled, moving away from her and reaching for the plate. 'Anyone would think you haven't eaten for a month.'

She gave an awkward laugh and helped herself from the plate. 'They're good. Did you make them?'

'Don't be ridiculous. I'm a man. I can cook the basics but I draw the line at mince pies. These are courtesy of my sister, who filled my freezer when she was here last.'

'Is that the same sister who is the mother of those children?' She glanced across at the photograph and he nodded.

'Jessica.'

Miranda sighed. What would it be like, she wondered, to have a sister to fill your freezer?

She ate another two and decided that any more would appear greedy so she stopped and snuggled back against the sofa. Suddenly she felt deliciously full and alarmingly drowsy.

'Five minutes,' she murmured, closing her eyes. 'Just five minutes and then I'm going to have to go home.'

And as she finished speaking, she fell asleep.

CHAPTER THREE

THE telephone woke him from a delicious dream of being wrapped in silky dark hair and kissed by a warm, soft mouth.

Cursing softly, still half-asleep, Jake reached out and answered it. 'Yes.'

'Mr Blackwell?'

He recognised the voice of the senior midwife on the obstetric unit and was instantly awake. 'Ruth?' He glanced round his living room and realised that he was alone. *Where was Miranda?* She'd fallen asleep and he'd covered her in blankets and then proceeded to fall asleep next to her. Only there was no sign of her now. And the weak, winter sunlight shining through the windows told him that it was morning.

'Jake—are you still there?'

Trying to ease the ache from his shoulders, he forced himself to concentrate on the phone. 'Yes, I'm here. What's happening?'

Was she using the bathroom?

'I've got a nightmare going on here, that's what's happening. I've just admitted a woman who was hoping for a home birth— fifth baby. But the last one was delivered by Caesarean section.'

Jake struggled to make sense of what she was saying. 'Fifth baby?' His brain was still foggy with sleep and his shoulders ached. He hadn't slept on a sofa since he'd been a student and now he remembered why. 'She doesn't sound like the best candidate for a home birth.'

'Which is presumably why she didn't register with anyone,' Ruth said wearily. 'She was staying with her parents for Christmas and she's just turned up here in labour because her mother-in-law has bullied her into it. Very stroppy. Hates hospitals. Hates doctors. I've managed to persuade her to let me check the foetal heart rate and there's some bradycardia. I'm not very happy about her really and I don't want to call Mr Hilton because I think she's going to be quite difficult to manage and you're good with difficult patients and he's not.'

Merry Christmas, Jake.

He closed his eyes and breathed out heavily. 'All right—what else?'

'You're not going to like the next bit of news.'

'I wasn't crazy about the last bit.' He smothered a yawn. 'Go on.'

'Lucy Knight's waters have broken.'

Lucy Knight? Jake rubbed his eyes with his fingers, trying to wake himself up. The penny dropped. 'Oh, hell—Lucy. She's only thirty-four weeks. When?'

'She called us early this morning.'

'Is she on her way in?'

'She's here already. Mr Hilton was prowling around and wanted to see her, but I said you were coming in today.'

'You're a star.' Having a colleague like Edgar Hilton was of dubious benefit. The man was a revered obstetrician with myriad publications to his name, but he was also renowned for his inability to let a mother labour without interference. It was a subject on which he and Jake disagreed at regular intervals. 'So is she having contractions?' He kept the phone to his ear as he wandered through to the kitchen, listening as the senior midwife outlined the situation. 'And you're sure it's amniotic fluid? OK—well, put her on the monitor and I'll be in as quickly as I can.'

'I feel guilty asking you. You're not supposed to be working today.'

Jake prowled round the kitchen, still holding the phone to his ear. *No sign of Miranda.* 'Don't be ridiculous, Ruth. It's my job.'

When had she left? During the night or early this morning?

'Well, even you're allowed a day off.'

'I had a day off. Christmas Day.' And it had turned out to be better than he'd ever hoped. *Finally, he'd met a woman who fascinated him in every way.* And now she'd vanished. Why had she vanished? He knew that she was interested in him too. Was it because he'd rushed her? Was that why she'd left? Pondering the facts, he reached for a jumper that he'd left over the back of one of the chairs. 'Give me ten minutes to shower and sort myself out here and then I'll be in.'

He replaced the receiver and sprinted upstairs, calling Miranda's name and checking in the bedrooms and the bathrooms. There was no sign of her.

She'd gone.

And he had absolutely no idea where because he hadn't had the sense to take her address. Hadn't seen the need, because he'd had no idea that she was going to perform a vanishing act.

Damn.

And now he had to go into the hospital because he didn't want to leave Lucy Knight to the tender mercies of Edgar Hilton and he didn't like the sound of the woman who'd planned to deliver her fifth baby at home. It promised to be a long and tiring day.

Cursing long and fluently, he showered quickly and then dressed and went to the kitchen to find his car keys.

Her bicycle had gone and there was a note on his windscreen that just said, 'Thank you.'

Thank you for what? Rescuing her? *Kissing her?*

No surname, no phone number, no address. Nothing to tell him where to find her again.

Miranda.

It was only the second time in his life that he'd felt instantly and powerfully drawn to a woman. The first had been Christy, and since then he'd virtually given up hope of finding anyone who interested him on anything other than a physical level.

Until yesterday.

Everything about Miranda had fascinated him. He'd always thought of himself as a man who understood women, but he'd found her complex and unpredictable. She'd shown strength and courage where other women would have panicked, but then she'd shown cynicism way beyond her years where other women would have been dreamily romantic. And what about her family? When he'd found her on the mountain, she'd said that she didn't have any family, but most people had some family somewhere. Had she fallen out with them? He frowned as he read the note again and then crumpled it up and stuffed it into his pocket.

He intended to find out. And he intended to find out why she'd left without leaving him her phone number or address. She'd felt as strongly as he did, he knew that for sure, so why the secrecy?

What did she have to hide?

What was she afraid of?

Muttering about the complexities of women, Jake drove towards the hospital, mindful of the icy roads.

He was going to track her down, he vowed as he drove through the gates of the hospital and pulled up in a space marked with his name.

Complex she may be, but there'd been a powerful connection between them and he wasn't about to let that go.

He strode onto the labour ward minutes later to be greeted by Ruth, the midwife who had phoned him.

He lifted a hand and tugged gently at the tinsel in her greying hair. 'Is that a new look?'

'It's my Christmas look,' she said primly, lifting a hand to protect the tinsel, 'and I don't welcome any of your usual sarcastic comments. You're lucky I'm even trying to look festive, given what's going on in this place at the moment.'

'Me? Sarcastic?' Jake went through to his office and frowned at the pile of papers on his desk. He'd only had one day off, for goodness' sake. How could so much paperwork have accumulated so quickly? 'So—how's our Lucy?'

'Scared,' Ruth said frankly, handing him a fat set of notes. 'You know what happened last time, although not here, of course, thank goodness. The baby was stillborn and she was utterly devastated. She's afraid the same thing is going to happen.'

Jake lifted his gaze to hers. 'We're not going to let that happen. I probably ought to warn you now that if her waters have broken then my threshold for inducing her is very low.'

'Usually you do expectant management.'

'Usually women don't have Lucy's history. She'll probably go into labour on her own anyway, but we'll keep a close eye on her. Just as a matter of interest, what's the bed state on SCBU?'

'They've got room,' Ruth said immediately. 'I checked earlier because I knew you'd ask me that question.'

'I'm that predictable?'

'You're that thorough.' Ruth's gaze softened. 'It's why you're such a brilliant obstetrician, Jake. You treat every woman as an individual case, regardless of protocol. And you don't miss anything.'

'Let's hope not. How's your staffing situation?' He knew that the whole hospital had been affected by the flu bug that was going around, and Obstetrics was no exception.

'It's been better but I've got a lovely bank nurse working

today. Sweet girl. Smiley and calm. She's going to be with us for a while, hopefully. At least over the holiday period.'

'Good. Jake nodded. 'Lucy needs someone calm.'

'You know that Lucy wants to have a vaginal delivery…'

Jake sighed and dragged his fingers through his hair. 'Yes, I know she does. Obviously it's what we all want. It's the way babies are supposed to be born.'

Ruth grinned at him. 'For an obstetrician, you're a revelation, do you know that?'

'I can't understand why you think I gain any enjoyment from increasing my workload,' Jake drawled, and she gave a little shrug.

'All I'm saying is that it's lovely to work with a senior doctor who is on the same wavelength. And Lucy feels it, too. Just knowing you were coming in calmed her down,' Ruth told him. 'She trusts you.'

Jake gave a wry smile. 'No pressure, then.'

'Your job is one long pressure,' Ruth replied as they walked down the corridor. 'I've put her in Suite 1 because it's more homely and I think she'll find it less stressful than some of the other rooms. She's not bleeding but she's had some funny pains off and on. They've got a bed on the ward if you want to keep her in.'

'Husband with her?'

Ruth nodded. 'Of course. And he's more anxious than she is.'

'Not surprisingly.'

Ruth paused outside the door. 'How was Christmas, by the way?'

For a moment Jake had a vision of a beautiful, mysterious woman with clouds of dark hair and a soft, tempting mouth that tasted as sweet as it looked. 'Christmas was interesting.'

Ruth raised an eyebrow. 'Meaning?'

'Meaning that it was interesting.' Not wanting to elaborate,

Jake pushed open the door of the labour suite and stopped dead. Miranda was sitting on the bed, talking to Lucy.

His Miranda.

He blinked and checked that he wasn't hallucinating. Same ebony hair, same pale skin and soft pink mouth.

The mouth that he'd kissed and explored in sensual detail the night before.

For a moment he just stared at her stupidly, trying to work out what she was doing there. To the best of his recollection, he hadn't revealed where he worked or what his job was so she couldn't possibly have followed him.

'This is Miranda Harding.' Ruth's curious expression told him that something of his shock must have shown in his face. 'She's a midwife and she's going to be doing bank work with us for a while.'

Midwife? She was a midwife?

'Hello, Miranda.' Somehow Jake managed to keep any trace of irony out of his tone and he noted the faint tinge of colour in her cheeks with interest. It was quite obvious that she wasn't pleased to see him.

He gritted his teeth. Well, of course she wasn't pleased to see him. If she'd wanted to see him, presumably she wouldn't have stolen away in the middle of the night without leaving a number.

What exactly was she afraid of?

They were going to have a conversation, he promised himself, sooner rather than later.

'Miranda, this is Mr Blackwell, one of our consultants,' Ruth murmured, her eyes still on Jake's face. Questioning. 'He's going to be looking after Lucy.'

Miranda cleared her throat but it was Lucy who spoke, cutting through the mounting tension in the room.

'Oh, Mr Blackwell, I feel so guilty, dragging you away

from your Christmas. It's Boxing Day. You should be at home with your family.'

'Don't feel guilty, Lucy.' Jake was still looking at Miranda. 'I'd finished all the food and that's the important bit.' With a huge effort he turned his attention to his patient, promising himself that he'd deal with Miranda later. 'You were fine when I saw you in clinic last week so when did all this start?'

'Christmas Eve. I did a bit of last-minute shopping with my mum and I had a bit of pain but I didn't really think anything of it. Then, this morning, my waters broke.'

'Plenty of movements from the baby?'

'Oh, yes.' Lucy nodded. 'I've been counting, just like you told me to.'

Jake smiled. He'd been monitoring Lucy right the way through her pregnancy, and he liked her a lot. 'But no pains?'

'Nothing since Christmas Eve.' Lucy frowned. 'We had a quiet day yesterday, ate too much turkey, you know the sort of thing. Then I had an early night but when I woke up this morning my waters broke all over the bathroom floor. Gushed everywhere. Very embarrassing thing to happen.' She chewed her lip, her eyes huge and anxious. 'It's bad news, isn't it? Is the baby going to come early?'

Jake's gaze was steady. 'Very probably, but we'll try and keep him inside you for as long as possible. The first thing I'm going to do is arrange for you to have a steroid injection. That will help the baby's lungs in the event that he's delivered early.'

'All right.' Lucy's hands were curled into fists in her lap. 'What else?'

'I'm going to run some tests and then I'll decide. You're going to need to stay in, I'm afraid, for now at least.' He turned to Miranda, his expression cool. 'Can you arrange for her to have 12 milligrams of betamethasone IM straight away? And contact the ward and arrange for a bed.'

She avoided looking him in the eye. 'Of course. Could you write the betamethasone on the chart for me?'

Why wouldn't she look at him? It wasn't as if they'd done anything except kiss. Was it really so embarrassing and awkward? He wrote on the drug chart and handed it to her.

'I'm going to keep an eye on you for a while, Lucy. See what happens. If there's no sign of any activity, I might let you go home tomorrow.'

'You're not going to induce me?'

'Not yet.' Jake's tone was both gentle and reassuring. 'If we can hang on another week, it would be better for the baby. Better a week in your tummy than a week in an incubator.'

Lucy gave a brave smile and a nod. 'Yes.'

He heard the catch in her voice and sat down on the edge of her bed. Her hands were still curled into fists and he took hold of them gently and uncurled them. 'Relax, Lucy.' His voice was sympathetic as he rubbed her hands between his and warmed them. 'I know you're worried but I'm not going to let you out of my sight until I'm satisfied that all is well.' He waved a hand around the delivery suite, his gaze sardonic. 'Enjoy the surroundings. Order room service.' He turned to Miranda who had stood up while he'd been talking to Lucy and now had her back to him. 'I want to do an ultrasound, please.'

Ruth stepped forward with a smile. 'I'll show you where we keep the machine, Miranda.'

Jake watched Miranda, wondering why she had her back to him. Then she slowly turned round and the reason became immediately clear. His eyes dropped to her waist and he inhaled sharply.

'Stop looking so shocked,' Ruth laughed, punching him on the arm in a teasing gesture. 'Midwives are allowed to be pregnant too, you know. In fact, the mothers love it. Shows we're capable of understanding what they're going through. Miranda is six months now. More than capable of doing a good day's work still.'

Miranda didn't look at him and Jake's mouth tightened.

She was pregnant.

How could she be pregnant? *And how the hell had he not noticed?*

He was an obstetrician, for goodness' sake. He dealt with pregnant women on a daily basis. And he'd had a woman who was six months pregnant in his house and he hadn't even noticed.

Well done, Jake. Good going. He closed his eyes briefly. The signs had all been there. The fact that she ate so much, her extreme tiredness, the fact that she burst into tears for apparently no reason…

But what had she been doing on her own in the mountains on Christmas Day? *And what had she been doing kissing him when she was six months pregnant with another man's baby?*

Angry with himself and even more angry with her, his jaw clenched and his eyes hardened.

He'd thought she was interesting and beautiful and appealing. It turned out she was duplicitous and lacking in morals. No wonder she'd made cynical comments about families. Clearly she had no sense of responsibility.

'Never known you speechless before, Jake,' Ruth teased, walking Miranda to the door. 'We'll just go and get the ultrasound machine while you pull yourself together.'

'Do you think the baby will be all right, Mr Blackwell?'

Aware that Lucy was looking at him expectantly, Jake pulled himself together and stood up.

'We're going to check everything, Lucy,' he assured her, managing a smile despite the turmoil inside him, 'and we're going to keep a very close eye on you. Leave the worrying to me if you can. It's what they pay me for. But I'm afraid you're spending the rest of Boxing Day in here with us.'

'I'd be too scared to go home anyway,' she confessed ruefully.

Miranda came back with the ultrasound machine and Jake resisted the temptation to drag her back into the corridor and demand an immediate explanation for her behaviour. That was going to have to wait until they were alone. But they would be alone, he promised himself, and they were going to talk, whether she liked it or not.

Where had the father of her baby been when she'd been spending Christmas Day at his house? Had they had a row? The guy must have been worrying himself sick. He knew he would have done if his wife or girlfriend had vanished without any warning.

His eyes slid to her neat little bump and he asked himself again how he could possibly not have noticed that she was six months pregnant. She was so slight.

But when he'd first seen her she'd been wearing a bulky waterproof jacket and then she'd changed straight into his jumper, which had been at least six sizes too large. Large enough to conceal a pregnancy.

Why? *Why would she want to hide something like that?*

Forcing himself to concentrate on his patient, Jake slid the transducer across Lucy's rounded abdomen and studied the picture on the screen. Later, he vowed, he'd get her on her own and find out what was going on.

'OK, everything looks fine with the baby, Lucy, but I want you to stay in for now, if that's all right with you.'

'Whatever you think.'

'I think that if your waters have broken, I want you where I can see you for the rest of the day,' Jake said calmly, reaching for some paper towels and wiping the jelly from her abdomen.

'That's fine by me. I don't want you to go off duty.' Lucy

gave a worried smile. 'I want you to sleep here in the room with me tonight!'

Ruth smiled. 'Oh, don't worry about that—the work I've got for him, he'll still be here at New Year, but he certainly won't be sleeping.'

Jake gently covered Lucy with a blanket and stood up. 'Stop worrying,' he said softly, and then turned to Miranda. 'I want her kept on the monitor for the time being and let me know if there's any changes. I'll be back to check on her when I've seen the other lady.'

Miranda nodded and he turned to Ruth. 'Where is she?'

'Room 2.'

Jake could see from the look on Ruth's face that she was expecting the consultation to be difficult, and the moment he walked into the room he knew that she was right. The couple didn't appear to be speaking but the atmosphere crackled with tension.

The husband was hovering helplessly in the background and the woman, Gail, was leaning over a beanbag and her face was pale and sweaty. The moment she saw Jake, her features tensed.

'I need to tell you straight away that I don't want to be here and I certainly don't want any intervention.'

'Of course you don't.' Jake's voice was calm as he walked across to her and pulled up a chair. 'I'm Jake Blackwell, one of the obstetric consultants. I gather you were hoping for a home birth so being in here must be rather a shock for you.'

'I've had three at home and one in hospital.' She glared at him and then winced as another pain gripped her. 'And I don't want to repeat the experience. It's all monitors and machines that beep at you. That isn't what nature intended.'

'I completely agree.'

She stared at him. 'You do?'

'Absolutely. My belief is that nature should be allowed the

upper hand, unless she appears to be getting things wrong which, I'm afraid, she sometimes does.' He turned to look at Ruth, his gaze questioning. 'Notes?'

'I've requested them from her hospital,' Ruth murmured. 'I'm going to get someone else to take Lucy to the ward and ask Miranda to come in here. I think she'd be helpful.' She slid out of the room, leaving Jake alone with the couple.

He looked at the CTG trace that Ruth had handed him and studied the pattern. Then he put the trace down on the table and concentrated his attention on Gail, knowing that he was going to have to handle her carefully.

'All right. I think honesty is the best way forward so I'm going to be straight with you.'

She tensed and glared at him with blatant hostility. 'You want to induce me so that you can have this room for the next poor woman—'

'I'm not given to inducing women unless the health of the baby is threatened,' Jake said smoothly, aware that Miranda had just entered the room. 'I've certainly never induced a woman to satisfy a staffing or bed need and I don't intend to start now.'

'I had three babies at home with no problems.' Her voice rose and her husband put a hand on her arm to calm her. 'And then with number four my placenta was low-lying so they had to take me in and I had a Caesarean section. And they were all totally useless! I had an infection and was really ill—'

'Oh, you poor thing.' Miranda hurried across the room. 'I can quite see why you wouldn't want to be here. You must be terribly anxious about it all.'

Jake looked at her and felt a flicker of admiration. She'd seen through the stroppy, angry exterior and seen the anxiety, just as he had.

'You obviously had a less than perfect experience last

time,' he said quietly, turning his attention back to Gail, 'and for that I'm sorry. It's always disappointing when childbirth doesn't go as nature intended.'

'It was a nightmare. I shouldn't be here.' Gail glared at her husband. 'And I wouldn't be if your mother hadn't forced the issue.'

'She didn't want you having a baby in her kitchen on Boxing Day, love,' her husband said awkwardly, running a finger around the neck of his jumper as if it was suddenly too tight. Gail tried to struggle to her feet.

'Well, I'm sorry if I'm inconveniencing everybody, but I just want to go home now!'

Miranda slipped an arm around her shoulders. 'Please, Gail, just stay and listen to Mr Blackwell. He'll take a look at you and make some suggestions. We're asking you to listen, that's all. No one's forcing anything on you.'

'I had three babies at home with no problems whatsoever.' Gail's voice rose as she looked at Jake. 'Give me one good reason why I shouldn't have this one at home.'

'Because having had a Caesarean section last time, you'll be at slight risk of the scar opening up,' he said frankly. 'And with your fifth baby you're more likely to have other problems, so it's safer for both of you if you're in an environment where we're geared up to help if necessary.'

'Intervene, you mean.'

Jake picked up the trace and leaned towards Gail. 'Look at this.' He ran his finger over the line on the paper. 'This tells me that your baby's heart rate was a bit slow here—and again here. I want to keep an eye on that.'

'There are always variations in heart rate,' Gail said immediately, her gaze challenging. 'At home they don't monitor it constantly so you don't know about it and you don't worry. And the baby is still fine when it's born.'

'Sometimes that's true.' Jake's voice was quiet. 'But are you willing to take that chance? What I'd like to do, with your permission, is ask Miranda to monitor you for a while so that I can get a better look at what's happening during each contraction.'

'You're just going to drag me into Theatre at the first opportunity and cut me open!'

Jake shook his head. 'If you want to check my records, I have a very low Caesarean section rate compared to the national average,' he said calmly, 'but I'm not willing to sacrifice a baby to keep that rate low. I can't promise you that I won't perform a Caesarean section if I think it's necessary, but I can promise you that we'll make the decision together. If everything goes well, there's no reason why you can't just quietly deliver your baby here. It's not home, that's true, but it's a comfortable room and we do our best to make it as relaxing as possible.'

Gail stared at him and then at her husband, who looked exhausted, stressed and totally out of his depth.

'Oh, hell, I don't know,' she muttered under her breath, and then her eyes slid to the trace again and she put a protective hand on her abdomen. 'You really think that the baby might be in trouble?'

'I don't know. We need to do some more tests.'

Gail hesitated and then gave a reluctant nod. 'All right. I suppose I'll stay. For now. But I don't want a stream of staff through here, staring at me or practising on me.'

'There won't be a stream of staff. Just me. I'm going to be staying with you,' Miranda assured her, and Gail gave a wan smile.

'I've heard that before. We both know that if my labour happens to run past the end of your shift I'll get someone else,' she said bitterly. 'I had three midwives in total last time I had the misfortune to deliver in hospital.'

'Well, that isn't going to happen this time,' Miranda said softly, putting a hand on her shoulder. 'I can promise you that, whatever happens, I will stay until you've had this baby.'

Gail looked at her and gave a disbelieving laugh. 'It's Boxing Day. You're pregnant yourself and you've got a family waiting for you. I should think it's bad enough working, let alone running into overtime.'

Miranda's gaze didn't flicker. 'I'm staying until you've had the baby. Now, if it's all right with you, I want to put you on the monitor and see what's happening.'

Something in the stiff set of her slim shoulders drew Jake's gaze but there was nothing in her face to reveal what she was thinking. Who was her family? Where was the father of her baby? Suddenly he wished Gail had chosen to be more direct in her questioning. He might have received answers to some of the questions buzzing around his head.

'I'll be on the unit if you need me.' He stood up and went back to his office to catch up on some paperwork, but every time he thought he was making headway he was interrupted.

He saw another patient for Ruth and then called the ward to check on Lucy.

When he looked up Miranda was standing in the doorway. Her gaze was wary and it was obvious that she would have preferred not to seek his help. 'Gail's progressing slowly. I presume you don't want to accelerate labour with oxytocin?'

Jake shook his head. 'There's some evidence that it increases the risk of rupture. How's the foetal heart?'

'Showing variable decelerations.' Miranda handed him a trace. 'Gail's complaining of pains, which might just be normal labour pain, of course, but I have a bad feeling about her.'

Never one to dismiss the instincts of a midwife, Jake looked at her. 'She had a lower transverse incision, which makes a uterine rupture less likely. And she's only had one previous Caesarean section.'

Miranda nodded. 'That's all true, I know, but her labour is slowing down and the baby's heart rate isn't as I would like it to be. And there's something about this pain she's complaining of that worries me. It just doesn't sound like labour pain.'

Jake dragged his eyes away from the smooth skin of her cheeks and concentrated his attention on the trace. Instantly he saw the problem. 'I'll take another look at her but it certainly isn't going to be easy to persuade her to allow us to intervene in any shape or form. Is she still as defensive as ever?'

'I don't think she means to be defensive. She's just very frightened.'

'There's often more to a person than meets the eye, isn't that right, Miranda?'

She had the grace to blush. 'Perhaps.'

'You and I are going to talk,' he said softly, and she straightened her shoulders.

'There's nothing to talk about.'

'There's plenty to talk about, but it will keep for now. We need to see to Gail.'

CHAPTER FOUR

WHY was it, Miranda wondered as they walked through the labour ward towards Gail's room, that every time she lowered her guard, it backfired?

When she'd made the impulsive decision to go back to Jake's house the day before, it hadn't occurred to her for even a moment that she'd ever see him again, let alone find herself working side by side with him.

And now he'd seen that she was pregnant and had jumped to all the wrong conclusions.

She gave a sigh as she pushed open the door to Gail's room. Well, she could hardly blame him for that, could she? He didn't know anything about her circumstances because she hadn't shared them with him. And she had no intention of sharing them with him.

It had been a mistake to go back to his house with him the day before. A luxury she should never have allowed herself. She'd been naive to think that she could just enjoy the moment and walk away.

She pulled herself back to the present and concentrated on supporting Gail, who was listening to Jake.

'I'm not happy with what I'm seeing,' he said gently. 'The baby's heart rate is slow and I'm worried about your scar.'

Gail stared at him defensively, a sheen of sweat on her brow and her eyes blank with pain. 'The scar will be fine. I've read enough to know that the chances of a uterine rupture are minimal and I'm not having another Caesarean section. I'd rather take the risk.'

'It's true that it isn't common for the uterus to rupture,' Jake agreed, 'but in certain circumstances it can happen. And the risk isn't just to your life, it's to the baby's life.'

Her fear and frustration barely contained, Gail's eyes filled and she looked away from him. 'I should have stayed at home,' she muttered, her voice clogged by the threat of tears. 'I should never have let them bully me into coming in. Everything would have been fine, then.'

'No, Gail. It wouldn't have been fine.' Determined to add her voice to Jake's, Miranda stepped forward and slid an arm round the woman's shoulders. 'I'm a huge advocate of home birth, but this is one baby that never should have been born at home. And I think, deep down, you know that.'

Gail sniffed. 'Where are you going to have your baby?'

'Oh...' Aware of Jake's glance in her direction, Miranda's face flamed. 'I don't know. I've only just moved into the area and I haven't had time to give it much thought yet.'

And she couldn't talk about it in front of Jake. It was too personal. *Too intimate.*

Before she could question her further, Gail pulled a face and placed a hand on her abdomen. 'Ouch! That hurt.'

'Another contraction?'

'It didn't feel like it.' The woman's face was pale and she grimaced again. 'Oh...'

'It could be the scar.' Jake stepped forward. 'I know it's the last thing you want, but I want to take you into Theatre, Gail. Just to be on the safe side.'

Miranda caught his gaze and knew instinctively that he was

starting to share her bad feeling. 'She's only three centimetres dilated,' she reminded him in a soft voice, and he nodded.

'I know. I want her in Theatre.'

'All right.'

Gail stared at him. 'I really don't know—'

'Gail.' His voice was urgent as he sat down on the edge of the bed. 'My job is to deliver a healthy baby from a healthy mother. You're not letting me do that job. I know it's hard for you but I'm asking you to trust me.'

'Well, it's just that I don't—' Gail broke off and gasped, one hand on her abdomen. 'Oh—what *is* that pain?'

'The trace is showing foetal bradycardia,' Miranda murmured, and Jake gave a decisive nod and turned as Ruth walked into the room.

'We need to deliver this baby right now and I want it done under general.'

Jake's swift glance said it all and Ruth hurried off to bleep the anaesthetist and prepare the theatre.

'What's happening?' Gail's eyes were wide with fear now and tears glistened. 'Oh, God, it's all going wrong, isn't it?'

Her husband stepped forward, his face pale and his eyes darting nervously to Jake, seeking reassurance.

'Gail, so far the baby is fine.' Jake's tone remained calm. 'But I think there may be a problem with your uterus. I have a suspicion that's what the pain is. I'm going to have to take you to Theatre. I'm sorry. I know it wasn't in our plans and I know it will be disappointing for you, but there's no other way. I don't want to risk the baby and I know you don't either.'

'I don't want an operation. Not like last time. I'm terrified of epidurals.' Hanging onto control by a thread, the tears spilled over from Gail's eyes and Jake took her hand in both of his, his blue eyes kind.

'I know you're worried,' he said quietly, 'but you have to

let me do what has to be done. I need to deliver this baby and I need to do it fast. And we won't do it under epidural. It will be under general. You'll be asleep.'

All animosity forgotten, Gail clutched his hand. 'I'm *so* scared.'

'You wouldn't be human if you weren't, but let me do the worrying.' Jake's voice was firm. 'I need you to trust me, Gail.'

Miranda swallowed at the kindness and confidence in his voice.

She was hopeless at trusting men and yet at this precise moment she'd trust Jake with her life, she thought to herself, and obviously Gail felt the same way because she gave a wan smile and a nod and reluctantly let go of his hand so that he could leave the room and prepare for the delivery.

Gail's husband was white with strain and Ruth guided him gently out of the room and showed him where he could wait.

Miranda stayed with Gail in the anaesthetic room, holding her hand until she was unconscious and mercifully oblivious to everything that was going on around her.

Meanwhile, Jake had changed and scrubbed and was waiting in Theatre.

He glanced up as they pushed Gail into the room.

'Right, folks, let's work fast.' He spoke to the anaesthetist. 'Have we ordered blood?'

'Six units of whole blood and I've requested a full blood count and coagulation studies. She's got two peripheral lines in and I've bleeped the haematology doctor on call.'

'Tell me when I can start.'

The anaesthetist checked his machines and nodded. 'Her blood pressure is dropping. She's bleeding from somewhere. You were right to bring her to Theatre—you'd better start.'

'Ruth, I want porters ready to fetch that blood and I want

the crash trolley in here.' Jake's voice was calm, 'I'm not taking any chances.'

Miranda watched while he swiftly and skilfully opened the abdomen and then made another incision in the fascia.

'Forceps.' Without lifting his gaze from the wound, he held out a hand and the theatre nurse immediately handed him forceps followed by scissors which he used to lengthen the incision and separate the muscles of the abdominal wall. Then he made an opening in the peritoneum and carefully examined the uterus.

'She's bleeding badly and I can't see where from—suction, please.' He held out his hand again and removed the clots. 'Uterine rupture of any degree is extremely rare,' he muttered, 'so why did it have to be on my shift and with a patient who wouldn't let me near her? OK—that's looking better. I can see what I'm doing now. Retractor.'

Miranda watched in fascination. She'd never seen a surgeon as slick and fast as Jake. His concentration was absolute, his fingers moving swiftly as he delivered the baby and the placenta.

She found that she was holding her breath and when the baby suddenly started crying there was a collective sigh of relief, but Jake's gaze didn't shift from the operation site. His responsibility towards the baby had ended with delivery. Now he was concentrating on the mother.

'There's significant blood loss,' he murmured, lifting the uterus out of the pelvis to determine the extent of the injury. 'Put 20 units of oxytocin in a litre of saline. I want 60 drops a minute until the uterus contracts. Clamp.'

The nurse handed him the instrument he needed and he moved with swift precision, clamping and ligating bleeding vessels and then using figure-of-eight stitches where necessary. Finally he was satisfied that the bleeding had stopped.

Miranda watched in breathless silence as he drained a hae-matoma that had formed and then examined the area again. 'Her previous Caesarean section was stitched with a single layer of sutures—a way of shortening the time in the operating room but it does increase the risk of uterine rupture. I'll do a double-layer closure this time.' His eyes still on the wound, he held out a gloved hand. 'I'm ready to stitch.'

The scrub nurse handed him the correct suture and he set about repairing the tear. 'More light,' he requested at one point. 'I need to see the ureter. Don't want to be stitching that. Right—clots here. Sponge, please.'

The nurse obliged and Jake carefully removed the clots.

Miranda stepped closer, her curiosity overcoming her reluctance to draw attention to herself. 'Is her bladder OK?' She knew that bladder injury was a very real risk but Jake gave a nod of his head.

'It all looks fine. And no signs of infection so I'm ready to close. The uterus has contracted. Reduce that drip to 20 drops a minute. How's that baby doing?' Finally, once he knew the mother was out of danger, he turned his attention to the paediatrician. 'Give me some good news, Howard.'

The paediatrician smiled. 'Little girl and doing very well indeed.'

'Apgar scores?' Jake's fingers flew as he stitched with equal measures of speed and skill.

'Eight, nine and ten.'

Miranda smiled with relief. The Apgar score measured neonatal heart rate, respirations, tone, colour, and reflexes immediately after delivery. Gail's baby had good scores.

Finally Jake finished and stepped back. 'All right. Well done, everyone. Thank you very much. Ruth, tell the ward to contact me if there are any signs of infection. Day or night, I want them to phone me. Gail has had a rough enough ride.

She doesn't need any more problems. And we need to redeem the reputation of the medical profession.'

Everything about him was calm and steady, Miranda observed as she watched him strip off his gloves and walk towards the swing doors. Just like the time he'd rescued her from the mountain. He assessed the situation and just did what needed to be done. Panic and Jake Blackwell clearly didn't go together. ·

He was an amazing doctor.

But it didn't take a genius to see that he was angry with her.

And who could blame him?

Dreading the inevitable confrontation, she took her time helping Ruth to clear up Theatre and then waited in the recovery room until Gail was well enough to be transferred to the ward.

It was nearing the end of her shift when she finally returned to the labour ward. There was no sign of Jake.

Weak with relief that she was going to be spared a difficult conversation, at least for the time being, Miranda found Ruth. 'Is there anything else you want me to do?'

'Are you joking?' Ruth gave her a smile. 'You've already worked far longer than you should have done, considering it's Boxing Day. I'm sure you have places you want to be. Go home.'

Miranda gave a wan smile. 'I'm fine.' Exhausted would have been a more appropriate word but she'd grown used to tiredness over the last few months. And there was no denying that the money would be very welcome. 'I'll see you tomorrow.'

'Marvellous. Thank you so much for today. You were my present from Father Christmas,' Ruth joked as she checked on the number of delivery packs. 'I was expecting to struggle through Christmas with no staff, and suddenly they called me out of the blue and said that they had a midwife available.'

'I was relieved to get work,' Miranda confessed, running

a hand over her bump and pulling a face. 'I thought you might not want me.'

And then she would have been in trouble because she needed every penny she could save. Pretty soon she wouldn't be able to work at all…

'You're fit and healthy. That's all that matters. See you tomorrow.'

Miranda grabbed her jumper and jacket and walked slowly to the set of railings where she'd left her bike. She was so tired, she wanted to cry. Her legs ached, her head throbbed and her eyelids drooped. All she wanted was her bed. At least she'd be too tired to notice the grimness of her surroundings, she thought as she walked across the badly lit car park. She doubted she was even going to find the energy to undress.

She'd just stooped to take the lock off her bike when a smooth male voice came from directly behind her.

'Running away, Miranda?'

Not having expected to see anyone, she gave a cry of alarm and covered her mouth with her hand. 'Oh—you frightened me.'

It was Jake and he was leaning against the railings, watching her, his handsome face cold and unsmiling.

'Why?' His tone was as chilly as the weather. 'Expecting someone else, perhaps? Your husband?'

Tall and broad-shouldered, his blue eyes glittered dangerously in the darkness and he looked nothing like a respectable consultant. *Nothing like the kind, reassuring man she'd seen calming Gail and Lucy earlier.*

The anger in his eyes was unmistakable and her heart gave an uncomfortable lurch.

She hadn't anticipated that he'd be angry when he discovered that she was pregnant, but neither had she anticipated the fact that she'd see him again.

They said that your sins always caught up with you and it

seemed as though her sin, although small, was currently biting at her heels.

She should never have gone home with him and she *definitely* shouldn't have kissed him.

She ignored the tension in his jaw and the question in his eyes and tried to turn the conversation to safe ground. 'You were amazing in Theatre.' She'd hoped that reminding him that they were colleagues would be sufficient to encourage him to back off, but his gaze didn't shift from hers.

'I don't want to talk about work, Miranda.' His blue eyes were hard. 'I want to talk about what the hell you were doing, spending the day with me yesterday—*kissing* me—when you're pregnant with another man's baby!'

She didn't even have enough energy to defend herself.

A freezing gust of wind howled across the car park and a few flakes of snow wafted past her face. She was cold, tired and she still had to cycle the two miles home. The last thing she needed was confrontation. And she didn't need to think about a kiss that she'd spent one whole night and day trying to forget.

'Can we talk about this another time?'

'No.' His voice was thin. 'We can't.'

'All right.' She turned to face him, so tired that her own temper started to bubble up. 'For a start, I didn't kiss you—you kissed me.'

'So this is my fault?'

How could she ever have thought he was a nice man? Looming over her now, he looked tough, intimidating and just about as far from nice as it was possible to be.

She was a lousy judge of men, she decided with no small degree of self-derision. Lousy.

'I didn't say it was your fault.'

'Good. Because I may have kissed you but you kissed me right back. What's your excuse? Are you going to blame the atmosphere? Or the alcohol you didn't drink? Where was the father of your baby while you were kissing me?!'

'Damn you, Jake!' Exhaustion and disappointment made her temper break loose. For a moment she'd thought he was different. Special. 'You know absolutely nothing about my life! And one kiss doesn't give you the right to moralise on a subject about which you know nothing!'

She swayed slightly and he swore softly and gripped the tops of her arms with strong hands.

'Look at you, you're exhausted! What are you trying to do to yourself, Miranda? Yesterday you were walking on your own in the middle of nowhere in lousy weather and today you've just worked a ridiculously long shift. You're pregnant. You should be looking after yourself and the baby.'

His words were the final straw. She *was* looking after herself and the baby. *She had to because there was no one else to do it.*

'I'm perfectly aware of my responsibilities towards the baby,' she spat, wriggling her arms out of his grip and glaring at him. 'That's why I turn up at work even though I'm exhausted. Not all of us have the luxury of being able to spend our pregnancy lazing around in bed. And my life is none of your business.'

'You keep making it my business.' He moved towards her, his blue eyes glittering in his handsome face. 'It was my business when you tried to half kill yourself on a mountain yesterday and it was my business when you spent the day with me and kissed me. And it was my business today when you were working on my unit.'

She backed away and wrapped her arms around herself to try and stop the shivering. She was going to have to find another job. *This was never going to work.* Suddenly she just wanted to go home. If the tiny flat that she'd rented could be classed as home. 'Fine. I made a mistake, walking on the mountains without checking the weather, I admit it. And I admit that I should never have gone home with you, but you wouldn't take no for an answer and it seemed harmless enough at the time. Obviously it wasn't, but you know what they say about hindsight.' She turned and pulled her bike away from the railings. 'Now, I need to get home.'

'On that?' He stared at her bike in disbelief and her answering glance was loaded with derision and disillusionment.

'Yes, on this. We're not all the fortunate owners of a Porsche, Mr Blackwell. And now, if you'll excuse me, I expect we'll see each other tomorrow.' Unfortunately. She was tempted to call the agency and ask them to send her somewhere else but she knew that there wasn't anywhere else. This was the only obstetric unit for miles around. And she wasn't in a position to move again. She had to think of the baby now. She had to put down roots—make a home for them both.

A feeling of warmth spread through her and a rush of protectiveness. The same feelings she'd had from the moment she'd discovered she was pregnant. Given the circumstances, she probably should have been appalled, but she'd been thrilled and delighted. *Excited.* Of all the things she regretted in her life, becoming pregnant wasn't one of them.

'That's it?' He reached out and gripped her handlebars so that she couldn't go anywhere. 'That's all the explanation you're prepared to give me?'

The warmth inside her faded. 'What do you want me to say?' She gripped the bike tightly, trying to ignore the insistent throbbing in her head. 'That I'm a slut who kisses men even though she's six months pregnant? There we are—I said it. I behaved badly.' Her tone was flippant and slightly bitter. 'I shouldn't have gone home with you and I shouldn't have kissed you.'

'Then why did you?'

'Because you were pushy and because I—' She broke off, struggling to explain something that she hadn't even managed to explain to herself. Why had she gone home with him? 'It was Christmas Day. I didn't want to be on my own.'

'Why would you have been on your own? Did you have a row with your husband?'

Husband? 'No!' She didn't want him thinking that of her. 'I'm not married.'

'Partner, then.'

Partner? What a joke. 'Mr Blackwell.' She tugged at the bike so that he was forced to let go. 'I think we should just forget the whole thing now. I'm grateful to you for rescuing me and giving me somewhere nice to spend Christmas Day. But it's history. Christmas has a way of doing funny things to people. If you don't believe me, just think about the increase in suicides and all the people who make utter fools of themselves at office parties. We all go a little mad at Christmas. And now I need to go home.' Before her aching, exhausted body gave up the ghost and slithered to the ground.

His mouth was set in a grim line. 'Is he waiting for you?'

Why was he persisting in this line of questioning? 'Does it matter?'

'I want to know what sort of man would let his girlfriend climb alone in the mountains in the middle of winter and then let her vanish for a day and a night without calling the police.'

The same sort of man that didn't care that he'd made a girl pregnant.

Miranda gritted her teeth and gave another shiver. She didn't want to think about him. He wasn't worth it. She and the baby didn't need him. They didn't need anyone. 'My life isn't your business.'

'You made it my business when you forced me to rescue you from a mountain and when you kissed me back.' He was glaring right back at her. 'You can't cycle home in this weather. Why isn't he picking you up?'

'Oh, for goodness' sake, why do you care? Goodnight, Mr Blackwell.' She tried to push past him but his powerful, athletic frame blocked her path and he muttered something under his breath and then lifted her bike.

'Come on, I'll give you a lift home. Your bike can go on the back of my car. It isn't the first time.' He strode across the car park with her bike and she stared after him in a mixture of misery, temper and frustration. *And consternation.*

She didn't *want* him to give her a lift home. She didn't want to give him the chance to question her further or find out anything about her.

'Miranda!' Having fastened her bike, he turned, his glance impatient. 'Get in the car before you freeze.'

Short of bodily wrestling the bike away from him she had very little choice but to stalk across to him and climb into his car. Again. Her mind was working overtime. She needed to find a way out of this situation and she needed to do it fast. There was no way that he could be allowed to drive her home. It would stimulate more questions that she had no intention of answering.

'All right, give me directions.' He slammed the door shut, slid into the driver's seat and started the engine. 'Where do you live?'

'Not far,' she said vaguely. 'Turn right out of here and then take the first road on the left.' She felt several wriggly movements from the baby and put a hand on her stomach with a soft smile. It was as if he or she was reminding her that she shouldn't give away too much.

Jake stared at her for a moment and then his mouth tightened and he reversed out of his space. 'You look pale.'

'Do I?' It was probably the shock, she thought numbly. The shock of seeing him again, mingled with the worry of having to reveal details of her life that she didn't want to reveal. Suddenly she was struck by inspiration. 'Take the second road on the right. That's it. If you drop me here, that's fine.'

He slowed the car. 'Here?'

'Yes.' It wasn't where she lived but he didn't need to know that. 'Thanks.'

He pulled up and removed the bike from his car, glancing at the row of large Victorian houses. 'Is this where you live?'

'Thanks for the lift,' she said quickly, ignoring his question and taking the bike. 'And I'm sorry about yesterday and everything. If it's OK with you, I'd just like us both to forget it ever happened. I'll see you at work, Mr Blackwell. Thanks a lot.'

'Hold on a minute, you can't just—' He was interrupted by his mobile phone and he cursed softly as he reached into his pocket and answered the call.

Silently thanking the hospital for choosing to call at that precise moment, Miranda climbed onto her bike, made sure that he wasn't looking in her direction and then silently pedalled away from him into the darkness.

Fifteen minutes later, in a very different part of town, she let herself into her tiny flat, propped her bike against the wall of the gloomy living room and yanked off her gloves.

Relieved that he obviously hadn't managed to follow her, she locked the door firmly behind her, dragged herself the few steps to the bed and sat down. She eyed the damp patch on the wall with resigned humour.

'It's a good job you're not born yet, hotshot.' She rubbed a hand over her stomach, talking to the baby as she often did. 'At least you can't see where we're living. I promise to do better than this by the time you make an appearance but, in the meantime, at least I'm saving money for us both.'

She pushed away thoughts of Jake's spacious, comforting living room. She wasn't going to think about his fabulous bathroom and she wasn't going to think about the flickering fire or the deep, comfy sofas. And she most definitely wasn't going to think about *that* kiss.

It had been a stupid, wild moment and it wasn't going to be repeated.

She could hardly blame him for being annoyed. He'd judged on appearances, and hadn't she done exactly the same thing herself in the past? Wasn't that why she was in this situation? The facts at his disposal suggested that she'd deceived him and she, of all people, knew exactly how that felt—remembered only too well the sharp, vicious pain of discovering the depth of someone's deception.

Part of her wanted to defend herself, blurt out the whole truth so that he realised just how wrong he was, but what was the point of that? It didn't matter what he thought of her, she reminded himself. In fact, it was probably a good thing that he had a low opinion of her. It would stop him pursuing her further.

She gave a laugh of self-mockery. What man in his right mind would pursue a woman who was six months pregnant? She toed off her shoes and wriggled her aching feet. Not a man like Jake Blackwell, that was for sure. He clearly lived in fairy-tale land. He saw a pregnant woman and assumed she had a caring partner somewhere. *If only...*

For a moment she remembered Jake's skill and kindness with the women on the unit. Then she remembered the warm, tumbling feeling in her tummy when he'd kissed her, and buried her head in the pillow with a groan. *Why* had she kissed him?

It was bad enough having been self-indulgent enough to go back to his house, but to have kissed him was *unforgivably* stupid. And now she was paying the price. Her long-dormant body was well and truly awakened. Her body and brain were disturbingly unsettled. *She wanted things she shouldn't want and could never have.*

She sat up and brushed her hair out of her eyes in a determined gesture. She needed to put Jake out of her mind. Tomorrow at work she'd be brisk and professional and she had no doubt that he would be the same. Now that he knew that she was pregnant, why would he take the trouble to pursue her?

They'd shared a kiss and now he was annoyed because he felt that she'd deceived him. And that suited her fine because she didn't want his approval. Really, she didn't.

By tomorrow the damage to his ego would have faded and she'd be just another member of staff. And that was what she wanted. Absolutely.

Too tired even to take her clothes off, she flopped back onto the pillow, pulled the duvet over herself and fell into a deep sleep.

CHAPTER FIVE

THE unit was already busy when she arrived the next morning.

'I can't believe the number of women who came in last night,' Ruth muttered as she checked the whiteboard and added another name. 'I'm going to need you in Room 3, Miranda, if that's OK. Daisy Priest. Really nice lady, but it's her first baby and she's a bit nervous. Her waters have broken but she's still only two centimetres dilated so I think you're in for a long one. Mr Hardwick is her consultant, but she's not very likely to need him.'

There was something in Ruth's tone that made Miranda give her a second look, but the older woman had already hurried on to the next topic. From her own point of view, Miranda was relieved that Jake wasn't Daisy's consultant. Not that he was likely to get involved in a normal delivery, but at least it meant that she was guaranteed a day where she didn't have to bump into him. A day to gather herself together after the conflict of the previous day.

'No problem.'

'Call me if you need any help. Oh, by the way…' Ruth gave a quick frown '…she has a doula called Annie, with her. Nice lady. She's been in here before.'

Miranda nodded, knowing that a doula was someone who

accompanies a woman in labour, giving her emotional support during childbirth. "OK. Thanks, Ruth."

'No problem.' Visibly stressed by pressure of work and lack of staff, Ruth hurried off to greet a woman who had just been transferred from the antenatal ward and Miranda walked down the corridor to find Daisy.

She was a woman in her twenties with a mass of curling blonde hair, and she was deep in conversation with an older woman who seemed to ooze calm and serenity.

Miranda introduced herself and Daisy looked at her anxiously.

'I hope you don't mind me bringing Annie, my doula. I know that not many women do, and—'

'That's fine,' Miranda reassured her quickly. 'Actually, where I trained in London, quite a few women used doulas. I think it's lovely for a pregnant woman to have the extra support.'

'It's just that I wanted someone familiar with me,' Daisy explained, 'and my husband Callum is hopeless with anything medical. Useless. He's downstairs in the shop, buying us a stock of magazines, because he couldn't stand witnessing a contraction. How pathetic is that?'

Miranda smiled and picked up Daisy's notes from the table. 'It can be very hard for a man to watch his wife in pain,' she said quietly, 'and I quite understand the need for a familiar and friendly face while you deliver.'

She knew from past experience that doulas were there to 'mother the mother' rather than offer advice on delivery and she had no problems at all with Annie being part of the process.

'I've read everything there is to read and watched everything there is to watch,' Daisy told Miranda, and then gave a grin. 'Don't look like that. The one thing that the books warn you about is that labour rarely goes according to plan. Annie keeps telling me that I've got to stay relaxed and go with the flow.

I'm glad she's here because, to be perfectly honest, I find Mr Hardwick, the consultant, really scary. He always seems cross.'

Miranda put down the notes she'd been reading. 'I haven't actually met him, but I'm sure he isn't cross. Perhaps just a bit serious. I see you're hoping for a water birth?'

Daisy nodded. 'I love the idea of being in the water. I swam every day in my pregnancy. One of my friends gave birth in water and she loved it. Do you think it's possible?'

'Absolutely, although we won't want you to get into the water too soon or it might slow your labour down. And we might ask you to leave the water for the actual delivery.' Miranda made a mental note to check on the hospital policy for water births.

'That's fine. I don't care about that.' Daisy screwed up her face and gritted her teeth. 'Ouch. That's really starting to hurt.'

'Remember your breathing, Daisy.' Annie put her arm round the younger woman's shoulders. 'Breathe through the contraction.'

Miranda slid a hand over Daisy's abdomen to feel the strength of the contraction and talked quietly to her as she gave a little moan of pain and clenched her fists. Finally she relaxed. 'It's going off now…' She breathed out heavily. 'Why did it sound so easy during antenatal class? They made you feel as though you could cope with anything, but the truth is that the pain takes you over.'

'Lots of women say that.' Miranda stood up. 'That was a pretty strong contraction. You might find the water comforting. Have you considered any other forms of pain relief?'

'I just want to try the water to start with,' Daisy said firmly, glancing at Annie for reassurance. 'I know that I might need something more and if I do then that's fine, but just for now I want to see how I go. I suppose I'm afraid that if I plan something else, I might grab it instead of managing.'

'So…' Miranda sat down on the chair next to the bed and gave a smile. 'Have you painted the nursery?'

Daisy gave a dreamy smile. 'It's perfect. You should see it. Primrose yellow with such pretty curtains…'

They talked and Miranda monitored her, and halfway through the morning she slipped out to talk to Ruth about the hospital policy on water birth.

'She's five centimetres dilated and her contractions are strong and regular now. I think she could go into the water if that's OK with you?'

'No problem,' Ruth said immediately. 'Daisy is a perfect candidate, but none of our consultants like the mothers to deliver in the pool. To be honest, Mr Hardwick doesn't like women to use water at all, but he's had to agree to it because of the pressure from women.'

'What about Mr Blackwell?' Miranda couldn't stop herself asking the question and then kicked herself when Ruth shot her a curious look.

'Jake? Oh he's perfectly relaxed about it. I've never met another doctor quite like him and I've worked with quite a few. He believes that women should labour in whatever way feels best for them. Such a contrast from a couple of his colleagues, who glance at their watches from the moment a woman walks through the door and then start reaching for the forceps.' There was a weariness in Ruth's tone that was hard to miss.

'Because they want to get women out as soon as possible?'

'Partly.' Ruth shrugged. 'And I suppose there's an element of control there. They want the woman safely delivered in as short a time as possible. Some obstetricians are nervous of litigation and are less inclined to take risks than others.'

'And Jake Blackwell isn't?'

Ruth frowned. 'I wouldn't say he takes risks. He's just very relaxed and confident and he puts the mother first. He tries to let women do what they were built to do. He has a very low rate of intervention. I'll tell you this much…' Ruth reached up and rubbed a name off the whiteboard with a scrap of tissue '…if I was having a baby, there's no one I'd rather deliver it. Talking of which, where are you having yours?'

'Oh…' Miranda blushed and placed a hand on her abdomen in a self-conscious gesture. 'I don't know, to be honest. I've only just moved into the area. Here, I presume, given that it's the only unit for miles around.'

'You should register with someone.'

'I know.' Miranda pulled a face. 'It's on my list of things to do. And I wouldn't know who to register with.'

Ruth dropped the tissue in the bin. 'Why don't you ask Jake? He's brilliant. The best, in my opinion. Tom Hunter is good, too, although not quite so approachable. If I were you, I'd go for Jake.'

'No, I couldn't possibly do that!' The words burst out before she could stop them and Ruth gave her a long, searching look.

'All right.' She spoke quietly. 'But you ought to register with someone. Are you carrying your notes?'

Still struggling from the emotional turmoil of imagining the intimacy of Jake delivering her baby, Miranda stared at her. 'What? Oh—yes. Yes, I am. But it's been a very straight-forward pregnancy. No problems at all.'

Except for the fact that her life was a total mess. But that probably didn't count, she assured herself. Physically she was fine and that was all health professionals ever cared about.

Ruth was still looking at her. 'Think about it,' she urged. 'As you say, if you're living around here then this is the only unit in the area.'

Miranda nodded. 'I'll do something about it, I promise.'

She and Ruth prepared the water and Annie helped Daisy into the pool.

Instantly the frown on her face faded and her eyes closed.
'Oh—that feels completely fantastic,' she murmured, as she
spread her arms out and slid further under the water.

At that moment her husband came into the room, clutching magazines and water. A tall man with glasses and a beard,
his tension was obvious as he looked at his wife.

'So how's it going?'

Still with her eyes closed, Daisy smiled. 'Perfect.'

Her husband breathed a sigh of relief and put the magazines down on the table. 'Can I do anything?' It was obvious
from his tone that he was hoping that the answer was going
to be no and Daisy chuckled.

'Just sit and talk to me for a bit.'

Miranda stayed with Daisy for the whole day, monitoring
the baby's heart with the waterproof, handheld Doppler and
generally offering support.

Towards the end of her shift she slipped out of the room
to give Ruth an update and found her talking to an older
man in a suit.

'This is Mr Hardwick,' Ruth said quickly. 'Mr Hardwick, this
is Miranda, one of our new midwives. She's looking after Daisy.'

The consultant made a disapproving sound. 'Is she nearing
the end of the first stage? I'm going out to dinner tonight and
I don't want to be disturbed.'

Miranda bit back the sharp response that flew to the tip of her
tongue. 'She's doing very well. She's in the water now and—'

He frowned. 'That will slow her labour down.'

Miranda took a deep breath. 'On the contrary, I've often
found that the relaxing effect of the water actually pushes
labour forward, providing the mother isn't put into the water
too soon. Daisy didn't go in until she was five centimetres
dilated and now she's—'

'I want her out of the pool for delivery.' Mr Hardwick's

mouth tightened. 'It's impossible to estimate blood loss in 600 litres of water.'

'Of course.' Miranda felt her hackles rise. 'There's nothing to suggest that this will be anything other than a routine, normal delivery. The foetal heart is—'

'Obstetrics is nothing if not unpredictable, young lady,' the consultant interrupted her again, his tone frosty. He then turned to Ruth. 'I'll be in my office for another hour and then I have a car picking me up.'

Without uttering another word, he strode off the labour ward and Ruth sighed.

'Sorry about that. Communication skills aren't his forte.'

'Nice for the mothers,' Miranda said dryly. 'Now I see why Daisy finds him scary.'

'Yes, well, Jake is on tonight so if there are any problems we'll get him to sort her out, quietly and competently, while Mr H. is eating his starter,' Ruth said quickly, picking up a set of notes and making for the door. 'How's she doing, anyway?'

'Fine. I don't anticipate any problems.'

She was to regret those words.

Daisy's labour continued smoothly and as she reached the end of the first stage, Annie and Miranda helped her out of the pool.

Daisy groaned and slumped over a beanbag. 'I'm going to kneel. It's what we agreed would be best and it's what I feel I want to do.'

'Fine. Use any position that feels right.' Opening a delivery pack and quickly snapping on a pair of gloves, Miranda examined the labouring woman. 'I can see the baby's head, Daisy. You're doing so well. It won't be long now.'

Daisy continued to push and the head was delivered but then immediately retracted.

It wasn't something that Miranda had ever seen before but she knew exactly what it meant and felt cold fingers of panic slide down her spine. Without hesitation, she reached out and hit the emergency buzzer behind Daisy's head.

'Daisy, you're doing really well,' she said calmly, 'but the baby's shoulders don't seem to want to be born so we just need a bit of help here.'

And she needed it quickly. There wasn't going to be any time to disturb Mr Hardwick's dinner. They had minutes to deliver the baby.

'I want you to turn all the way over and back onto all fours—Annie and I are going to help you.'

She knew that such a manoeuvre might help dislodge the baby, but in this case nothing happened and seconds later Ruth hurried into the room, closely followed by Jake.

'She's had two contractions with no restitution—Turtle's sign—and having her on all fours hasn't worked,' Miranda told them quickly.

Without any further questioning, Jake immediately took charge.

'We'll try the McRoberts manoeuvre. I need you on your back, Daisy, and I need you to stop pushing—can we get her onto the bed, please?'

Ruth and Miranda quickly helped Daisy onto the bed and flexed and abducted her legs while Jake washed his hands and pulled on a pair of gloves.

He applied supra-pubic pressure then did something magical with his hands and the baby slithered out, screaming and bawling.

'Little girl, Daisy,' Jake said calmly, clamping the cord and handing the baby to the mother, as relaxed as if it had been a perfectly normal delivery.

It was only then that Miranda realised that she'd been holding her breath. The tension left her in a rush and her knees suddenly felt weak.

As if sensing her state, Jake gave her a gentle smile. 'Everything's fine. Good job, Miranda.'

She swallowed, grateful for the praise but not at all sure that it was justified. He was the one who'd delivered the baby, and with a minimum of fuss and bother. He'd been so calm that it was quite possible that Daisy had no idea of just how serious the situation had been. Suddenly she was swamped by uncertainties and insecurities. What if he hadn't been just down the corridor? What if they'd had to call Mr Hardwick away from his dinner? He never would have arrived on time.

'She's so beautiful,' Daisy breathed, just as the paediatrician hurried into the room.

'Did someone bleep me?'

Jake glanced up briefly. 'Everything's fine here, Howard, but, given that you've made the trip specially, perhaps you'd be good enough to take a look at the baby for us,' he said easily, focusing his attention back on the delivery of the placenta.

Daisy released the baby reluctantly and the paediatrician checked her over and pronounced everything to be fine. An hour later mother and baby were transferred to the ward. It was three hours after Miranda's shift should have ended.

Drained and exhausted and more than a little troubled by the events of the day, she walked slowly towards the changing room and dragged on her coat and scarf.

Wondering how on earth she was going to find the energy to cycle home, she pushed open the door that led to the stairs and then stopped. Jake was standing there, his broad shoulders leaning against the wall, blue eyes narrowed as he watched her.

'I've been waiting for you—you've just worked a ridiculously long day. Again. Are you all right?'

She almost laughed. She was so far from all right that it wasn't true, but she could hardly tell him that, could she? 'I'm fine.'

'You're a liar.'

She lifted a hand and tried to rub away the nagging ache in her forehead. 'If you want a rehash of last night's conversation, I ought to warn you that this isn't a good time. I know you're mad with me, but—'

'I'm not mad with you.'

'Last night you—'

'Last night I was angry, yes,' he admitted, 'but you have to admit that I had a lot to take in. I've had time to think about what you said and you're right, of course. Your life is none of my business but, for some reason that I don't entirely understand, I keep wanting to make it my business.'

'Jake—'

'I'm worried about you.' His voice was firm and masculine and his gaze was disturbingly intent. 'You shouldn't be working these hours when you're six months pregnant. I hope when you get home, he's spoiling you and feeding you decent food.'

Miranda thought of the contents of her fridge and gave a wan smile. 'Of course.'

Something flashed in Jake's eyes and he straightened. 'Come on, then. The least I can do is drop you home again.'

She glanced at him, startled. He hadn't actually dropped her home the night before, but he didn't know that, of course.

Too tired to argue with him, she followed him down to street level and watched in weary silence as he secured her bike to the back of his car.

Without speaking, he took the same route that she'd given him the day before and pulled up in the same street. Then he looked at her with a strange gleam in his eyes.

'Are you going to tell me the truth now?'

'About what?'

'Well, about where you live, for a start.' His tone was pleasant. 'I know it isn't here.'

Her spine straightened. 'I don't know what you mean.'

'Oh, I think you do.' He switched off the engine. 'You don't live here, do you, Miranda?'

She stared at him. 'I—'

'After I finished on the phone last night, I went looking for you. I knocked on every door in this street but no one had ever heard of a midwife called Miranda.' His gaze didn't shift from her face. 'Funny, that, don't you think?'

She swallowed hard. 'Jake, I—'

'So then I started to ask myself why you'd lie about where you lived.' His voice was steady and calm. 'It's obvious that you're involved with someone and that's fine, but I would like to know why you're lying to me. Why not just tell me the truth?'

'I'm not lying. I haven't lied once—'

'We're sitting outside a house where you don't live. What's that if it's not a lie?'

She looked away from him. 'I'm not used to confiding in people.'

'Giving me your address counts as confiding?' His tone was mild and she turned back to look at him.

'All right, you can take me home. But then I want you to leave. I'm not prepared to answer questions and I don't owe you any explanations.'

Jake pulled up outside the dimly lit block of flats and felt a shiver pass through him. In the darkness the whole area was threatening and unsavoury, and he knew from experience that daylight didn't improve it at all.

It was rough and dangerous and left him with one burning question that needed answering.

What on earth was Miranda doing, living in a place like this?

It seemed that the longer he spent with her, the less he knew about her life.

'Thanks for the lift.' She undid her seat belt but his hand closed over hers before she could open the door.

'Not so fast.' Her hand was slender and cold and he felt it tremble slightly under the pressure of his. Suddenly he knew she was hiding something. Something big. 'I'll see you to your door.'

'There's really no need. I can—'

'I'll see you to your door.' His mouth set in a grim line, Jake released her hand, opened his own door and walked round the car to help her out. 'Or are you afraid that your partner is going to give me a black eye?'

He was testing her reaction because he'd come to the conclusion the previous night that she didn't have a partner, and his suspicions were proved correct as she hesitated fractionally and then her slim shoulders sagged.

'I'm on my own.' Her voice was so soft he could barely hear her. 'No one is going to give you a black eye. But I still don't need you to walk me to the door.'

'Indulge me.' In fact, she looked so exhausted he wondered whether he should carry her, but he managed to stand aside as she walked towards the steps and led him up two flights.

'This is where I live.' She took a key out of her pocket. 'Thanks for bringing me home. I'll see you tomorrow.'

She pushed open the door and he caught a brief glimpse of damp patches and threadbare carpet.

It was enough to make up his mind. There was no way he was leaving her here without at least understanding what was going on.

He followed her into the room, resisting her feeble attempts to close the door on him with a gentle push of his shoulders. Once inside, his gaze bordered on the incredulous as he glanced around the gloomy room. 'What are you doing, living in a place like this?' He winced suddenly, aware that his words were insulting, but then he decided that there was absolutely no way that she could possibly think that her living conditions were anything other than awful.

It explained a great deal. It explained why she'd hesitated over using the word 'home'. No one in their right mind would refer to this flat as 'home'.

She lifted her chin. 'It's fine.'

He eyed the huge damp patch on the wall. 'Miranda, it's miserable.'

'I'm saving my money. And now I'd like you to leave, please, because—'

'I'm not going anywhere.' He pushed the door shut behind him and noticed that it made very little difference to the freezing temperature. The place bordered on the uninhabitable.

'Jake—'

'I can't believe you're living here. And I'm not leaving until you tell me why.'

She sighed. 'It's cheap.'

'I can believe it.' His expression was grim as he stared at the carpet. 'Is that the most important factor? Why do you need to save your money? Why isn't he supporting you?'

'Who?'

'The guy who made you pregnant. You might not still be with him, but at the very least he has a responsibility towards his child.' Anger tore through him and suddenly he wanted to plant his fist through the damp, mouldy walls.

Her eyes narrowed dangerously. 'I don't need anyone's support, Jake. I can look after myself.'

'But it's not just you, is it, Miranda?' His eyes dropped to the smooth swell of her stomach. 'It's the baby, too.'

'The baby is fine and, please, don't judge me. You don't know anything about me and you couldn't possible understand.'

'I happen to want to understand. Did he leave you?' He

knew that he probably shouldn't be asking but he couldn't help himself. He just knew that he couldn't leave her here like this. 'Is that what happened?'

She dragged off her coat and dropped it on the bed. 'Why do you care?'

He exhaled sharply, forced to admit that it was a reasonable question. And one he was having trouble answering. 'I care. Let's leave it at that.'

For a moment his eyes held hers and then she looked away. 'He was never here. He left as soon as he found out about the baby.'

'Honourable guy.' He couldn't keep the sarcasm out of his voice and wanted to kick himself when he saw the pain in her eyes. 'Damn, I'm sorry.'

'It's fine.' She sounded so tired that he wanted to gather her up and hug her. *Take her away from all this.*

'Miranda—'

'It really doesn't matter. I'll see you tomorrow, Jake. Thanks for the lift.' She walked through to the tiny kitchen. It was so small that she could barely turn in it and he decided that whoever had designed the flat should be made to live in it for a day.

'You think I'm going to leave you here?' He leaned against the doorframe and watched as she put the kettle on and pulled open the fridge—a fridge that was empty except for a box of eggs and one small carton of yoghurt. It was the final straw. 'Go and pack your things.' He said the words quietly and she turned with the yoghurt in her hand, her expression startled.

'Pardon?'

He couldn't blame her for looking surprised. He felt surprised, too. Wondering whether he'd gone mad, he folded his arms across his chest.

'I said, go and pack your things. I'm taking you back to my house.'

She pushed the fridge door shut. 'Don't be ridiculous.'

He tried to lighten the atmosphere. 'Sweetheart, you're the only woman I've ever made that offer to, so think hard before you turn it down.'

The brief flash of laughter in her eyes assured him that she hadn't lost her sense of humour.

'I think you're the one who probably needs to think hard. If it's seduction on your mind, Mr Blackwell, I think you've chosen badly.'

What exactly was on his mind? He had absolutely no idea. He just knew that there was no way he could leave her in this place, any more than he could have left her on the mountain. 'Come with me.'

She sighed and put the yoghurt down. 'Are you always this stubborn?'

'Yes.' He watched her steadily. 'On second thoughts, where's your suitcase? I'll pack for you.'

'Jake—'

'I'm not leaving here without you. It's as simple as that.'

'This is ridiculous.'

He smiled placidly, pleased by his decision. It felt right. 'No. It's just the way it is. Pack, Miranda, or I'll carry you out of here wearing only the clothes you're standing in, and we both know that my clothes are far too big for you.'

The reminder of the last time she'd worn his clothes brought a faint flush to her cheeks and he felt something stir inside him.

Never in his life had a woman posed so many questions. *And never had he so badly wanted to discover the answers.*

'Has anyone ever told you you're a bully?'

'I'm not a bully. I just know what I want and I'm very good at getting it.' In this case he knew what he wanted but he didn't understand why he wanted it. He valued his personal space more than anything else in his life. No matter who he dated, *no matter how hot the relationship,* no woman had ever moved into his house.

'I know what I want, too, and—'

'You're too exhausted to have the first clue what you want.'

She gave a weary smile. 'You might be right about that. I just want to lie down for five minutes.'

He wondered whether he should point out that she looked as though she needed a lot longer than five minutes but decided against it. 'Just pack, Miranda, and in under half an hour you'll be lying in a deep bubble bath with a soft, comfy bed awaiting your arrival.'

Something close to longing flashed into her eyes. 'You make it extremely hard to say no.'

'That's the general idea.'

She walked towards him. Without her shoes she barely reached his shoulders and he stared in fascination at her delicate bone structure and silky, dark hair. She was a woman of contrasts. Who would have thought that underneath that fragile, feminine exterior lurked the strength and determination of a lioness? She was the most independent woman he'd ever met.

She lifted an eyebrow. 'You're blocking my door and I need to pack for an overnight stay.'

Relieved and elated but unable to identify exactly why, Jake decided to get her out of there before she had time to change her mind. 'Pack for longer than that. I'm not bringing you back here until the place has been remodelled. I'm surprised you haven't gone down with some vile disease.'

'I'm tougher than I look.'

'Evidently.' He stood to one side and she wriggled through, her cheeks flushing again as their bodies touched.

Visibly flustered, she walked away from him, grabbed a

bag and stuffed a few things inside. 'I'm ready.' Her eyes flickered with uncertainty. 'I still think this is ridiculous.'

'Not ridiculous.' He took the bag from her and gave her a gentle push towards the front door, eager to get her into his car before she had time to change her mind. 'Sensible. And be careful on those stairs. Don't fall asleep on your way down.'

CHAPTER SIX

FOR the second time in a week, Miranda lay in a deep, warm bath full of bubbles in Jake's gorgeous house.

Deep down she knew that she probably shouldn't be here. She should have put up more of an argument. But Jake wasn't a man to take no easily and she hadn't been able to find the energy to protest.

And who could blame her for that?

What woman in their right mind would chose squalor over luxury, even if it was only for a short time? She was so exhausted that her whole body was shrieking with protest and at that precise moment she wasn't sure that she even had the energy to climb out of the bath. And she felt desperately worried about everything that had happened with Daisy. Had it been her fault? Should she have been able to anticipate the problem that had arisen?

A knock on the door interrupted her thoughts and Jake appeared, carrying two mugs. 'I brought you sustenance.'

Miranda gave a soft gasp of embarrassment and slid further under the bubbles. Why hadn't she remembered to lock the door? 'You can't come in here!'

He pushed the door shut with his shoulder. 'Why not? You're tired. I was worried about you. I wanted to check you hadn't fallen asleep in the bath.' Totally unrepentant, he put the two mugs on top of the laundry basket, then reached for a towel and held it out to her. 'Get out now while you're still awake and you can drink the hot chocolate I made you.'

'Hot chocolate?' With only her face showing through the snowy bubbles, Miranda stared longingly at the mug. 'Is that the same sort of hot chocolate you gave me on the mountain?'

'The very same.' He'd changed out of his suit into a pair of jeans and a soft, casual shirt that had obvious been washed repeatedly. He'd pushed the sleeves up to the elbows to reveal strong forearms dusted with dark hairs. 'Drink it now and by the time you're dressed, dinner will be ready.'

'You've cooked?'

'Not exactly.' He grinned and gave a shrug. 'I had some help from the local pizza company. Full of calories, I know, but you look as though you could do with building up.' His eyes lingered on her face. 'Are you all right? You look worried.'

He was observant, she had to give him that. 'I'm worried that I did all the wrong things with Daisy,' she blurted out suddenly. 'Should I have spotted a problem sooner?'

'Is that why you're frowning?' He sat down on the chair next to the laundry basket. 'The simple answer is, no, it certainly wasn't your fault. Why would you think it was?'

'I've never seen shoulder dystocia before,' she confessed. 'I've heard about it, of course. Who hasn't? But I've never actually seen it. I keep wondering whether I missed some important signs earlier. Perhaps if I'd spotted something, it wouldn't have happened.'

'Don't be too hard on yourself.' His tone was firm. 'A significant proportion of cases have absolutely no identifiable risk factors. You know that as well I do.'

Miranda was still running through the entire nightmare in her mind. 'Perhaps I should have done something differently when I saw the head retract. I tried left lateral then I tried putting her on all fours and then I moved her through 180 degrees but it didn't work.'

His gaze was steady. 'You did all the right things. And you called for help immediately, which is the most important thing of all.'

'But perhaps I should have tried the McRoberts manoeuvre first, instead of putting her on all fours. Will you explain something to me?' Miranda chewed her lip. 'Doesn't lying her on her back just narrow the pelvic outlet?'

'It corrects sacral lordosis and removes the sacral prominence as an obstruction.'

'So you basically have more space?'

Jake grinned and lifted one of the mugs to his lips. 'That's the theory. Unfortunately not all babies are entirely familiar with the theory.'

'Yes, well, that's my other worry. What if it hadn't worked? What then?' Miranda was thoroughly absorbed. 'You don't think there's value in performing an episiotomy presumably?'

Jake shook his head. 'The baby is impacted under the bony structures of the pelvis and the episiotomy will only deal with soft tissues. Knowing that you'd already had her in left lateral and on all fours, if the McRoberts manoeuvre hadn't worked then I would have tried to deliver the posterior arm, but obviously that isn't without risk.' He leaned forward and handed her the second mug of chocolate. 'Now, stop worrying and drink something. You must be starving. You did well today.'

Grateful for the frothy mountain of bubbles that at least afforded her a reasonable degree of privacy, she sipped the chocolate, warmed by his reassurance. 'I finally met Mr Hardwick.'

'And that was doubtless an uplifting experience.' His soft

drawl made her wonder how on earth the two consultants managed to work side by side as colleagues when their approach to obstetrics was so dramatically different. They probably didn't really work together much, she mused.

'He was rude.'

Jake nodded and finished his chocolate. 'Sounds fairly typical. He trained in an age when consultants were considered gods who dealt out instructions that people followed without question. These days we tend to favour discussion with the patient.'

'If you hadn't been in the hospital, what would have happened to that woman?'

'Well, strictly speaking, Hardwick wasn't on call so he didn't have to be there.' Jake suppressed a yawn. 'It all comes down to whether you want to hang around if one of your patients is in. Hardwick tends to keep an eye on his private patients and ignore his less well-heeled clients.'

Miranda frowned. 'That's awful.'

'Is it?' Jake lifted an eyebrow and his gaze was faintly sardonic. 'Would you want him around when your baby is delivered?'

Miranda shuddered. 'Most definitely not.'

'I rest my case. Talking of which, if you haven't chosen an obstetrician yet, you should speak to Tom Hunter. He's brilliant.' Jake glanced at his watch and stood up. 'Pizza delivery imminent. You'd better get dressed, unless you fancy wrestling with mozzarella in the bath.'

She slid further into the water. 'I can't get dressed with you standing there.'

He rolled his eyes. 'Miranda, I'm an obstetrician. I've seen pregnant women before.'

'You haven't seen me.'

His eyes locked with hers and she felt colour seep into her cheeks. It was the warmth of the water that made her body heat, she told herself hastily. Nothing more. She knew better than to fall for any man, let alone a man like Jake. He was single for a reason and she had no intention of becoming another notch on his belt.

She almost laughed at her own thoughts. As if Jake would truly be interested in her! She was six months pregnant with another man's child, for goodness' sake. She didn't exactly fit into the box entitled 'Uncomplicated Relationships'. Not to mention the fact that he probably didn't even find pregnant women attractive…

When he'd said that she was beautiful and had kissed her, it had been on Christmas Day, before he'd found out that she was pregnant. Things were very different now.

Furious with herself for allowing her thoughts to drift down that path, she glared at him. 'Leave me in peace and I'll get out of the bath.'

He took the empty mug from her. 'Fair enough. I'll meet you downstairs in five minutes. Any longer than that and I'm coming back upstairs to find you.'

'Has anyone ever told you that you're controlling?'

He smiled and strolled towards the door. 'Frequently. Blame it on the job. Occasionally I'm required to make instant, unilateral decisions. Sometimes that spills into my personal life.'

She watched him leave, a small, regretful smile on her face. He was an indecently attractive man but it wasn't his just his looks that made her stomach curl. It was his strength and his confidence.

And she shouldn't be noticing or caring. Didn't she ever learn?

Determined not to dwell on his attributes, determined to

forget that amazing kiss, she pulled herself reluctantly from the warm, soothing bath and wrapped herself in the fluffy, warm towel.

He heard her come into the room and turned, his eyes lingering on her flushed cheeks and the soft curve of her mouth. Dressed in pyjamas, with her hair secured on top of her head with a clip, she looked impossibly young and vulnerable and he felt something clench deep inside his gut.

Carefully hiding his reaction, he pulled out a chair and waved a hand. 'Sit down. I didn't know what you liked on pizza so I ordered everything.'

She peeped into the box and laughed. 'So I see. As an obstetrician, aren't you supposed to be preaching the sermon of optimum nutrition?'

'A little bit of what you want is good for you and I've decided that what you need most is calories and comfort.' He pushed the box towards her. 'Eat. Do you want a plate?'

Ravenous, she shook her head and reached into the box. 'No point.' She chewed and gave a moan of delight. 'Oh, this is delicious.'

'Good.' He watched the way her small pink tongue sneaked out and licked her lips and suddenly found himself in the grip of a vicious attack of lust. 'So—tell me your life story.'

She stopped chewing. 'Sorry?'

Cursing himself for having disturbed her meal, Jake decided that, having done so, he may as well push on with his questioning. 'I want to know what's happened to the father of your baby. You accused me of jumping to the wrong conclusion and I'm sure that you're right. So give me the facts. That way, I won't do it again.'

'You're very direct, aren't you?'

'I think it's better that way.' He trapped her gaze with his. 'It prevents misunderstandings.'

She gave a slightly cynical laugh. 'Does it?'

'I think so. Who is he, Miranda?'

She hesitated. 'I suppose I owe you an explanation so I'll tell you, and then I don't want to talk about it any more.'

'You don't owe me anything,' he said calmly. 'But I want you to tell me.'

'Why?'

Good question. 'Because you look like someone who needs a friend? So that I can track him down and black his eye for leaving you to struggle like this?'

'I'm not struggling.' She gave him a fierce glare and he fought back a smile, remembering how independent she'd been on the mountain. She clearly had a thing about looking after herself and yet she looked so young with her dark hair still damp from the bath and a slice of pizza in her hand.

Far too young to be a single mother with no support.

'Don't stop eating,' he said quietly. 'You need the food. Tell me who he was, Miranda.'

Ignoring the pizza in her hand, she chewed her lip and stared miserably at the kitchen table. 'Saying it out loud makes it even worse.'

He leaned forward and eased the slice of pizza from between her fingers.

'Eat.' He slid the pizza between her teeth and she gave a wan smile before obediently biting off a piece.

'I met him in a chat room on the internet.'

What was a beautiful woman like her doing, resorting to chat rooms on the internet? 'And?'

She shrugged. 'His name was Peter and he seemed nice. We chatted about all sorts of things. He liked all the same things as me—it was uncanny really.' She shook herself. 'Anyway, we spoke on the phone a couple of times and then we arranged to meet. He told me he was thirty-eight, which is a bit old, I suppose, but I wasn't worried.'

'So you met?'

'In a pub. He was good company and I…' She flushed. 'And I suppose the truth is that I was so lonely that I didn't bother asking the questions I should have asked.'

Jake felt more questions surge up inside him. Why was she lonely? Did she have no friends or family? With a determined effort he limited his question to one. 'What happened?'

'We went on a few dates and then, after about a month, he confessed that he'd lied to me and that he was actually forty-eight, not thirty-eight. I was really shocked. Not because of his age,' she added hastily, 'but just that he'd deceived me. I couldn't understand why he just hadn't told me the truth right from the beginning.'

Jake gritted his teeth. 'And why didn't he?'

'He told me that he was afraid I wouldn't want to meet him if he'd been honest about his age.'

Jake pushed the pizza box towards her. 'Eat another slice before you tell me the rest.'

'How do you know there's more?'

'Because it's written all over your face.'

She chewed slowly on the pizza and then sucked her fingers. 'We went out for a few more weeks and he persuaded me…' She blushed. 'I mean, I was obviously willing and—'

His appetite suddenly gone, Jake abandoned his slice of pizza. 'He persuaded you to go to bed with him.'

'Yes.' She sat back in her chair and closed her eyes briefly. 'I really want to tell you that I was madly in love with him but if I'm honest I think I was just incredibly lonely. And maybe that's why I didn't pick up any of the signs. I suppose I didn't want to see them.'

'What sort of signs?'

'He always called me, I was never allowed to call him

except on his mobile and that was usually switched off. We only ever met when he suggested it—'

'Because he was married?'

She stared at him, stricken. 'Is it that obvious to you?'

Clearly it hadn't entered her head. 'You're giving me all the facts,' he pointed out gently, 'whereas you were only in possession of half of them and then only what he chose to give you.'

She shook her head. 'You've no idea how many times I've gone over and over it in my head, wondering why I missed the clues. It seems so obvious now, but at the time—'

'Passion can be a powerful emotion.'

'There wasn't that much passion.' A faint colour touched her cheeks. 'In fact, I—' She broke off and he frowned.

'What?'

'Nothing.' She gave him a smile that looked more than a little forced. 'Anyway, the rest is pretty obvious. I discovered I was pregnant. He was completely horrified and suddenly produced a picture of his blonde wife together with four matching children. And that, as they say, is the end of the story.' Her tone was light but he saw the pain in her eyes.

'And how did you feel about being pregnant?'

'At first panicky and very alone.' She let out a long breath and gave a soft smile. 'And then pleased. I know that sounds weird, but I was pleased. It just felt sort of…right. I can't really explain it.'

'He owes you maintenance at the very least.'

'I don't want anything from him.' She sat up in her chair, dignified despite the pyjamas and the damp hair. 'I'm used to managing on my own and that's what I'll do. The only difference is that now there are two of us to look after.'

'So why the Lake District? What about your family?' *Why was she used to managing on her own?*

Shadows flickered across her pretty face. 'I don't have any

family,' she said flatly, standing up quickly and helping herself to a glass of water. She kept her back to him. 'I decided to move right away from London so I picked the Lake District because I've had a picture of it in my mind for as long as I can remember. I always loved poetry at school.'

'Poetry?' His own mind was elsewhere, sifting carefully through information. There was something about her answer that didn't seem quite right. Or rather, there was something about the way she'd answered that hadn't felt right. He knew instinctively that she was lying. But why would she lie about family? Had they fallen out because she was pregnant? Was she embarrassed about her family?

'Wordsworth.' She turned to face him, still holding the glass of water. 'He lived here, you must know that.'

'Of course.' He gave her an apologetic smile. 'It's just that I was born here and you tend to take it all for granted after a while.'

'Maybe.' Her tone was wistful. 'Well, anyway, it sounded like an idyllic place. A good place to bring up a child. And not as expensive as London.'

He wanted to know more about what had happened to her family.

It was clear that, if her family were alive, they wanted nothing to do with her. *Or she wanted nothing to do with them.* Jake tried to imagine sticking a pin in the map and then deciding to build a life in a strange place. Tried to imagine what it would be like to have no roots. 'All right, I can understand you choosing the Lake District, but what made you choose that terrible flat?'

'It was all there was at the time and it was cheap,' she said simply. 'It's just me on my own and when the baby comes I'm not going to be able to work for a while so I don't want to waste any of it now. I'm going to look for something else soon. Somewhere I can move to after the baby is born.'

His eyes narrowed. 'How much are you paying in rent?'

She named a figure that seemed exorbitant for one dark room full of damp patches but he managed not to let his jaw drop. 'Right. Move in with me and you can save even more money.'

'You can't be serious.'

'I'm perfectly serious. Why not?' He waved a hand around the house. 'This place is far too big for me and you'd be much more comfortable here.'

'No.' Her voice cracked and something fierce flashed in her eyes. 'I don't need anyone's help. And I don't depend on anyone.'

She was ferociously independent and he sensed that if he didn't handle the situation with enormous care, she'd be back in her damp flat before he had time to dispose of the empty pizza box. He leaned back in his chair, stretched his legs out and kept his voice calm and steady. 'That's good, because I don't want you to depend on me. I'm just suggesting that you move into one of my spare rooms. You can pay me the same rent you're currently paying your landlord.'

'Absolutely not.' But he'd seen the brief hesitation and took instant advantage.

'Why? You're prepared to pay rent to a total stranger in return for a room.'

'That's different.'

'How is it different?' His voice was gentle and he watched her face for her reaction. 'Is it different because we kissed?'

She put the glass down and looked away from him. It was clear that, given the chance, she would have pretended that it hadn't happened. 'It wasn't a real kiss. It was Christmas Day, we were both lonely and—'

'Attracted to each other?'

Colour seeped into her cheeks. 'You can't possibly be attracted to me.'

'No?' The fact that she hadn't denied her own attraction to

him gave him more satisfaction than he would have believed possible. He wondered if he dared risk moving towards her but decided against it. 'Why can't I be attracted to you?'

'I'm six months pregnant.' *With another man's baby.* The words hung in the air, unsaid, and he gave a patient smile.

'And?' His gaze didn't shift from her face. 'None of the books I studied said that pregnancy changes a person. You're still you.'

'A very fat version of me.'

The fact that she suffered from all the usual insecurities suffered by pregnant women made him want to smile. 'You're a midwife. You should know that most men find their wives extremely attractive during pregnancy.'

'I'm not your wife.'

His desire to smile faded. He should have been relieved about that. Instead, he found himself thinking how amazing it would be if she was his wife. He'd have the right to snuggle up with her and kiss the frown away from her beautiful face. 'That's true, but—'

'I'm not anyone's wife and I don't ever intend to be.' The fire was back in her eyes. 'I don't want a family.'

Was this just about the man who'd lied to her or was there something more to her comment?

His eyes slid from her fierce gaze to her softly rounded abdomen. 'I hate to tell you this, sweetheart, but you're about to become a family, whether you like it or not.'

She placed her hand on her stomach in an instinctively defensive gesture. 'That's entirely different. I want this baby, but I don't—'

'There's no such thing as a typical family, Miranda.' He took a gentle nudge at her fears and prejudices. 'Everyone creates something different. Family is a pretty generic word for people living together and trying to make it work in the best way they can.'

'Is that right?' There was a weary cynicism in her eyes that lit the fire of his own anger. He didn't know what had caused the pain. He just knew that it shouldn't be there.

He decided to shift the subject slightly. 'Are you going to carry on giving donations to your crooked landlord or are you going to give me the money instead?'

'You're serious about renting me a room?'

He didn't want to take her money at all, but he knew that there was no other way she'd even consider the possibility. 'Very serious.'

She was silent for a moment, her head tilted to one side, her damp hair sliding out of the confines of the clip and over one shoulder. 'All right.' She said the words slowly, as if she wanted to see how they sounded. 'But I'll move out when the baby arrives.'

'Why would you do that?'

'Because you don't need a screaming infant keeping you awake at night. And because I can't lodge here for ever. I need to find somewhere permanent that I can turn into a home.'

He realised with a stab of shock that he wanted her to make her home here. *With him.*

Startled by his own thoughts, Jake lifted a hand to his forehead and rubbed at the frown lines. This was ridiculous. He'd only known her for a couple of days. The humour of the situation wasn't wasted on him. He'd lost count of the number of women who had dropped hints about moving in with him. He'd developed various strategies for gently but firmly locking his door with the woman on the outside. So why did he suddenly want to lock the door and keep Miranda on the *inside*?

'Fine.' He knew that his thoughts would have her scurrying hard back to her damp-ridden, gloomy flat without a backward look so he kept them to himself. 'Consider this a base until you find something more suitable.'

'It's very generous of you.' She fiddled with her hands, clearly troubled by something. 'I still don't understand why would you do this for me.'

'Does there have to be a reason?'

'Isn't there always?' She gave a cynical laugh. 'I'd be guessing at the sex aspect if it weren't for the fact that I'm six months pregnant.'

'There's a great deal more to my motives than sex.' His gaze was direct. 'OK, I'm not going to lie to you, Miranda, because you've obviously heard enough lies. The truth is, I don't exactly know why I want you to live here. There was something between us from the first moment we met on Christmas Day. When I woke up and found you gone I was frantic—frustrated. Then, when I discovered you at work, I felt light-headed until you stood up and I saw that you were pregnant. I've always had a rule that I never tread on another man's toes, so I was prepared to walk away even though I felt as though something important had been snatched away from me.'

Her dark eyes were huge. *Wary.* 'Jake—'

'Let me finish.' He stood up and walked towards her. 'Then I discovered that you're on your own. That I'm not treading on anyone's toes. And that changes everything, Miranda. Why do I want you to stay here? Because I can't let you go, it's as simple as that. I'm not sure what that means, but I'd like to find out.'

'I'm six months pregnant.'

'That doesn't change the person you are.'

'This is ridiculous, Jake—'

'Is it?' He saw the shock in her eyes and in a way it mirrored his own feelings because normally he backed away from women, didn't pursue them. It was ironic, he reflected, that the first time he was truly interested in a woman she was six months pregnant, fiercely independent and wary of men. With a faint smile of self-mockery he recognised that some of the women he'd dated would view his current situation as nothing more than poetic justice.

She stared at him and the tension in the room rose to agonising levels.

'I—I don't really know what you're saying but I don't want a relationship, Jake. Not with any man. I'm not trying to create a family.'

He smiled. 'As I said, you've got yourself a family, Miranda.'

'Well, it's just going to be me and the baby and that's fine by me.'

Why? he wondered to himself. Was it just because of the baby's father or was there more to it than met the eye? Something to do with her own family.

'You're worn out,' he said softly, deciding that it was best to end the conversation before he did something that might frighten her off. 'Go to bed, Miranda. We can talk tomorrow.'

'But you can't just—'

'Don't complicate the simple,' he advised. 'You're sleeping here tonight. Any more than that we can discuss at another time.'

CHAPTER SEVEN

'I DON'T think you should drive me to work,' Miranda said the next morning as she sipped the cup of tea Jake had made for her and nibbled on a piece of toast.

'Why not?'

'Because people might notice and talk. And that would be embarrassing.'

She'd been awake for most of the night, thinking about what he'd said. *He hadn't wanted to let her go.* Even while most of her was backing off, deafened by alarm bells, a small part of her was shiny with happiness.

'Coming from a woman who rides a heap of rust in public, I find it hard to believe that you care about what people think.' There was laughter in his eyes and she looked away, wishing that his smile wasn't so compelling.

He smiled at everyone, she reminded herself firmly. It was just the kind of man he was. You felt as though the smile was only for you, but it wasn't.

She had to be careful. Very careful. It would be foolish and dangerous to allow herself to dream.

'That's entirely different.' She put her empty mug into the dishwasher and then turned to face him. 'I'm pregnant, Jake. People will make the same assumptions about me that you did, and I don't want that. I don't want people thinking that I'm dishonest or unfaithful or any of the other things people assume when they see a pregnant woman with a man who isn't her husband.'

He gave a shrug, his expression unconcerned. 'As you told me on Christmas Day, what people see on the outside rarely resembles the inside so what does it matter? Let them gossip.' Evidently indifferent to the views of others, he strolled towards the door and held it open for her. 'Come on or we'll be late.'

She stared at him with mounting frustration. She was so used to taking charge of her own life that she wasn't sure how to deal with Jake.

But she decided that this wasn't worth an argument so she slid into the warmth and comfort of his car and squashed down the uncomfortable feelings bubbling up inside her. This was all wrong, she knew it was. What exactly did he want from her? And what exactly did she want from him?

Nothing, was the short answer to that. There was no way she'd ever consider entering into a serious relationship and a fling wasn't her style.

She had no opportunity to ponder the question further because once they arrived on the labour ward they were so busy that they had no time to discuss anything except the professional.

She felt as though she was on her feet all day and she was more than a little relieved to find Jake lounging by the doorway at the end of her shift, waiting to take her home.

Deciding that this was definitely not the time to argue with him, she slid gratefully into his car, pushing aside the horrible suspicion that people were watching them.

He was right. What did it matter? And why did she care? She, of all people, who knew only too well that outward appearances were entirely deceptive.

He drove her to her old flat and stood while she cleared out the rest of her things. She carried them to his car and then hunted in her pocket for the keys.

'I just need to deliver these back to the landlord.'

'Tell me which flat he lives in. I'll do it.'

'I can—'

'You're tired. Why waste energy walking up the stairs again when all you have to do is point me in the right direction and I'll do it for you?'

'He lives in the flat directly beneath mine, but I need to give him notice and explain to him that—'

'I'll explain,' Jake said, prising the keys from her fingers and heading back towards the building.

She ought to have argued with him, she knew that. It wasn't good to let people do things for you when you could perfectly well do it yourself. But he was right when he said that she was tired.

It was only when he slid back into the car and dropped an envelope into her lap that she realised that she'd actually dozed off for a few minutes.

'What's that?' Muzzy-headed from lack of sleep, she picked up the envelope and gasped as she saw the amount of money inside. 'Where did this come from?'

'Your landlord.' Jake started the engine and glanced over his shoulder before pulling away from the kerb. 'I explained that you were living with me now and he apologised profusely for the state of the property that he's renting to you and immediately returned your deposit and last month's rent as a goodwill gesture.'

'You spoke to the landlord?'

'That's right.' His eyes were fixed on the road. 'Very reasonable chap.'

There was something about the grim set of his mouth that

made her wonder and then her gaze dropped and she saw the red mark across his knuckles. 'You hit him! Oh, my God, Jake…'

'He walked into my hand.'

She covered her mouth with her hand, appalled. 'What's come over you?'

'I don't like people who take advantage of other people.' He glanced in her direction, his eyes glittering dangerously. For once there was no trace of humour in his gaze, just grim determination and a hardness that she hadn't seen before. 'Once we'd had a good chat, he saw sense.'

'How dare you interfere?' She was outraged. 'Jake, I didn't ask you to get that money for me!'

He pulled into the drive of his house and switched off the engine. 'The guy is a crook, Miranda.'

'It doesn't give you the right to hit him.' She undid her seat belt with shaking hands. 'I—'

'What's the matter?'

Her heart was banging against her chest. 'You really need to ask me that question? You just beat someone up and—'

'I didn't beat anyone up.' His voice was weary. 'He said some things I didn't like. Things he shouldn't have said. He's a bully, Miranda. A sleazy, nasty bully.'

'*You hit him.*'

Jake ran a hand through his hair. 'He attacked me, Miranda,' he said quietly. 'Accused me of taking away his business.'

Self-defence? She relaxed slightly and the pounding of her heart slowed. 'He hit you? I'm sorry.' Her voice was little more than a whisper. 'It's all my fault. I shouldn't have let you go in there.'

'Better me than you. Next time choose your landlord with more care.' Without waiting for a response from her, he opened the car door and walked towards the house.

She caught up with him in the kitchen. Looking at his stiff, icy profile, Miranda felt frustration and something else that she couldn't quite identify. A tiny part of her felt warm and cosseted. No man had ever defended her before. Maybe it shouldn't have felt good *but it did*.

He was only trying to help and she'd been rude and churlish. He'd been injured, standing up for her, and all she'd done had been to yell at him.

Suddenly ashamed of herself, she wrapped her arms around her waist and took a deep breath. 'I'm sorry,' she began, and he muttered something under his breath, before turning to her with a smile.

'No, I'm the one who should be sorry. I'm used to women who like to be pampered. You're the most independent person I've ever met. I thought I was doing you a favour.'

'You *were* doing me a favour. I hate that man—he makes my flesh crawl. It's just that I don't want you to feel sorry for me.'

'I don't.' His voice was soft. 'But you're a friend and it's natural to want to help a friend, isn't it?'

Miranda bit her lip. 'I don't know. I suppose if I'm honest, I've never really had a close friend before.'

'Are you joking?' He reached into the fridge for a beer. 'Women always have close friends.'

'Do they?' Miranda pushed away thoughts of her childhood and sat down at the kitchen table. 'I suppose I've always found it hard to be close to people.'

He studied her face for a moment and then smiled. 'Any chance of some first aid for my knuckles?'

She rummaged in his freezer for an icepack and fussed over his hands. 'Does it hurt badly?'

'If I say yes, will you kiss it better?'

She shot him a warning look. 'Be careful or I might damage your other hand.'

* * *

As the days passed Miranda felt nothing but pleased that she'd agreed to move in with Jake. In the warmth and comfort of his house, she slept better. In fact, there were several occasions when Jake had to wake her in the mornings.

She knew that, at some point, she was going to have to find somewhere to live once the baby was born, but she was so busy at work that all she wanted to do when she arrived home was collapse in a heap and sleep until her next shift.

And Jake made it easy for her to do that.

He was easy to live with, she discovered, and after that first night he'd kept the conversation friendly but impersonal.

Which was a good thing, she told herself firmly as she slid out of bed on a Saturday morning a month or so after she'd first moved in. She didn't want anything else.

Anticipating a slow, lazy day, she dressed in comfortable clothes and went downstairs to the kitchen to find Jake frying bacon.

'It's a lovely day.' He glanced towards her. 'Fancy a walk?'

After her first, disastrous foray into the mountains, he'd taken her to the mountain rescue base and shown her all the equipment they used in rescues and talked to her about safety. She realised again how fortunate she was that he'd been the one to find her on Christmas Day. Since then he'd found walking gear that fitted her and had insisted on taking her on some gentle hikes.

She slid a hand over her rounded abdomen. 'You fancy delivering a baby in the wild, Mr Blackwell?'

'You know me.' He gave her a wicked grin as he slid crispy bacon onto a plate. 'I love a challenge.'

She stared at the bacon. 'Is that for me? Because I can cook my own breakfast and you don't have to—'

'I don't have to wait on you.' His tone was patient. 'I know that, Miranda, and I'm not waiting on you. I was making breakfast for myself so adding a few extra rashers of bacon seemed like common sense.'

It sounded logical, put like that. 'I'm going to be the size of a small bus.'

'You have no flesh on you whatsoever,' he said dryly, dropping two slices of bread onto her plate and putting a jug of coffee in the centre of the table. 'That bump is all baby. Am I allowed to pour your coffee or does that offend your independent streak?'

'I know you're laughing at me but I won't depend on anyone.'

'You can relax. I don't want you to depend on me. Just for the record, you're cooking dinner tonight.' He poured coffee into two mugs and pushed one across to her. 'There we are. You should put milk in it. You need building up.'

She patted her stomach and there was humour in her eyes. 'You want to have to refashion all your doors just so that I can pass through them?'

'As I said, that bump is all baby.'

'Big baby, then.'

'Does that worry you?' He bit into his own sandwich and she looked at him, thinking, not for the first time, that he was incredibly astute. She saw it over and over again at work and not just among the women he delivered. He noticed when a midwife was slightly off colour, he knew that Delia in the staff restaurant was having trouble with her hip. He didn't miss anything and she really liked that about him.

Men were supposed to be useless at picking up signals and yet Jake seemed to notice everything.

'Honestly? A bit, yes. I suppose all women are apprehensive about delivery.' She picked up the sandwich and nibbled the corners. 'But I'm sure it will be all right. I took your advice and saw Tom Hunter. He's a nice guy.'

'Everything all right?'

'Yes, seems to be. I'm boringly healthy. Low blood pressure, plenty of movements.' She felt a little embarrassed discussing it. 'He didn't anticipate any problems.'

'He's a good obstetrician.' Jake sipped his coffee and grinned. 'Not as outstanding as me, of course, but I couldn't deliver your baby.'

'Why not?'

His eyes locked on hers. 'Because I'm emotionally involved and that isn't a good thing. Obstetricians have to be able to take a step back.'

His words made her insides shift alarmingly. 'Why are you emotionally involved? I'm just your lodger.'

He studied her face for a long moment, his blue eyes revealing nothing of his thoughts. 'If you've finished your breakfast, I think we should go for that walk. Exercise is good for you. If Tom didn't mention that fact then he should have done.'

'Jake—' she couldn't let the subject drop that easily '—we've been living together for a month now and you haven't mentioned—' She broke off and he smiled.

'The fact that there's this amazing chemistry between us?'

She blushed. 'After a month of living with me you've probably discovered that I'm a long way from being your ideal woman. I'm stubborn and independent and I fall asleep when I'm not working—'

'I'm assuming that the sleep thing will improve once the baby is born, and I happen to like your independent streak.' He stood up. 'Let's leave the clearing-up until later. It's February and you, of all people, know how changeable the weather can be. The sun's shining at the moment so we should make the most of it.'

Aware that he'd changed the subject, she followed him to the door, feeling as though the conversation was only half-finished.

'Jake—'

'Miranda.' He turned to face her, his eyes gentle. 'Are you sure you want to pursue this line of questioning? If you ask me, I'm going to be honest about how I feel and you'll be obliged to tell me that the relationship isn't going anywhere and then I'll argue with you and that will ruin our walk. So let's drop it for now.'

For now?

He was implying that he still had feelings for her, and yet…

She bit her lip, knowing that he was right. Whatever he said, she was going to back off.

'Get your boots on.' Jake pushed them towards her. 'I'll do them up for you.'

'I can do them myself, just about.' She slipped on another thermal layer and pulled on a jumper and then her coat. 'I'm boiling.'

'That's because you're in my house. It's freezing outside. We won't stay out for long and we'll do something flat so that it isn't strenuous.'

'What do you think I am?' She frowned as she fastened her boots, determined not to show him what a struggle it was. 'Pathetic?'

'No. Seven months pregnant.' He stepped forward, zipped up her jacket and handed her a hat. 'Wear that.'

'I'll get hat hair.'

'Women.' He rolled his eyes and walked towards the door. 'Better hat hair than hypothermia, sweetheart. Wear it.'

He drove to a lake that she hadn't visited before and parked the car. 'We'll just walk around the shore path. Very gentle and easy.'

It was a perfect clear day, crisp and cold but fresh and invigorating. The snow crunched underfoot and Miranda stamped her foot down into virgin snow. 'Don't you just love that?' She couldn't hold back the grin. 'Being the first person to touch the snow?'

'Just as long as the mark is caused by your foot and not your bottom.' He took her arm. 'I know I'll be on the receiving end of a lecture about your independent nature, but hold onto me or you might slip and break something. Perhaps we shouldn't have come.'

She lifted an eyebrow. 'You think I've forgotten how to walk?'

'No. I think the ground is slippery and your weight distribution has shifted.'

'You're just looking for an excuse to touch me.' She was teasing but the look in his eyes made her smile fade.

'I don't need an excuse, Miranda,' he said softly, his eyes burning into hers. 'When I think the time is right, I'm going to touch you and we won't be by a frozen lake when I do it.'

Suddenly she found it difficult to breath. 'Jake—'

'We agreed not to get serious today.' He stroked a hand down her cheek and then turned away, adjusting the rucksack that he always carried on his back. 'Come on, walk. But hold my arm so that you don't slip.'

Feeling slightly weak and shaky, she did as he instructed, her fingers curling into the solid swell of his biceps. She wanted to ask what he meant but she was afraid of stirring up something she wasn't able to handle.

They walked for about half an hour and Jake stopped and pulled out a flask. 'It's cold today. The temperature is dropping. I wouldn't be surprised if we have more snow.'

'Is the lake really frozen?'

'Only around the edges. It's very deceptive. The ice is extremely thin. Last year we had to rescue two children who thought it would be fun to skate and fell in.'

'Oh, my goodness.' Miranda took the hot drink from him gratefully. 'How did you get them out?'

'We balanced logs on the ice and used the ropes from our climbing gear.' They drank and talked and then Jake stuffed the flask back in his backpack. 'Have you finished? We probably ought to be making a move.'

'Let's go a bit further before we turn back. It's so lovely to be outdoors.'

His blue eyes gleamed. 'Can this possibly be the same girl who was wearing trainers and not much else when I met her on Christmas Day? I thought you were a city girl.'

'Not any more.' She shook her head and glanced around her wistfully. 'I never want to go near a city again. The baby and I are going to live here happily ever after.'

'That sounds lonely.'

Aware of his searching gaze, she blushed slightly. 'I don't think so. As you once said to me, families come in many different guises.'

'I meant, lonely for you.' He stepped closer to her. 'Aren't you a little young to be dismissing the male species from your life?'

It was impossible to look away and her heart fluttered and skipped at the look in his eyes. 'I'm trying to keep my life simple.'

'Is that right?' Somehow his head had moved nearer to hers and now his mouth hovered, tantalisingly close. She stared up at him, hypnotised by the slightly slumberous look in his eyes. His jaw was rough with stubble and he looked more handsome than any man had a right to look, and her body's reaction was as intense as it was instant.

Her legs wobbled, her insides tumbled and swirled and that was before he even touched her. Perhaps he knew the effect he was having on her because the last thing she saw before his mouth came down on hers and her eyes drifted closed was lazy amusement in those wicked blue eyes.

Then he kissed her and she slipped into his kiss as easily as she had that first time, on Christmas Day.

No wonder she hadn't been able to resist him, she thought dizzily. His mouth was warm and skilled, his kiss slow and so erotically seductive that all the power drained out of her legs. Unable to stand without support, she clutched at his jacket and felt his arms slide around her as he pulled her against him.

Lost in a mysterious world of sensation that she'd never before discovered, it was only after he'd reluctantly released her that she realised his mobile phone was ringing.

Swearing fluently under his breath, Jake kept one arm around her and used the other to dig deep in his pocket for his phone. 'Yes?' His response was less than enthusiastic and she could understand why. She was ready to strangle the person who'd interrupted them. Or perhaps she should be grateful, she said to herself as she eased herself away from the pressure of his arm, taking advantage of the fact that all his attention was now on the phone. It seemed that it was all too easy to give in to Jake's charms. No matter how hard her lesson, she seemed to have no willpower where he was concerned.

'Problem, I'm afraid.' Jake snapped the phone shut and dropped it into his pocket, his eyes narrowed as he stared down the path ahead of them.

'You're not on call. Mr Hardwick is supposed to be covering this weekend.'

'It isn't a baby. It's a woman who's slipped by the lake and broken her ankle.'

'Which lake?'

Jake was squinting into the distance. 'This lake. You and I are the advance party, sweetheart.'

'You want me to help you with a mountain rescue?' It was hard to keep the irony out of her voice and he turned to her, his eyes gleaming with appreciation.

'Actually, we've always thought that an extremely pregnant woman would be an asset to the team.' He trailed a finger down her cheek in an affectionate gesture that had her heart racing. 'We're not up a mountain and I don't need you to do any rescuing, but I do have to go and help and I'm not prepared to leave you here or let you walk back to the car on your own.'

Wondering what it was about him that had such a powerful effect on her, she adopted a frosty tone. 'You think I'm helpless?'

'No, I think you're very pregnant and this walk probably wasn't a sensible idea, but it becomes even less so if you go back on your own. What if something happens, Miranda?' He frowned. 'It isn't about independence, it's about common sense.'

She thought for a moment and nodded. 'All right. I'm not going to argue with you.'

'You're not?'

'No. What do you want me to do?'

'She dialled 999 a few minutes ago and the leader of the mountain rescue team thinks that she's not far from here. If he's right then we should be able to stretcher her down the valley and meet the ambulance at the road.'

'I only see one problem with that.'

He started walking along the path. 'What's that?'

'We don't have a stretcher. Or do you carry one in your magic bag, along with the hot chocolate?'

He laughed. 'My colleagues will be bringing the stretcher, the ambulance will wait at the end of the path and our job is to administer first aid and make sure she's comfortable.'

'They're going to walk along here, carrying a stretcher?'

'It breaks into pieces.'

'Oh, yes, I remember now. You showed me one that evening you took me around the mountain rescue centre.'

They walked for another fifteen minutes and then Jake waved a hand. 'There she is. I see her. By that tree.'

'She looks all huddled up.' Miranda frowned. 'I hope she's all right.'

'Let's find out, shall we?'

They reached the woman and she gave a wan smile. 'I didn't think anyone else would be stupid enough to walk along here in this weather, but I see I was wrong.'

'I'm Jake Blackwell, I'm from the mountain rescue team.' Jake dropped down so that he could examine her ankle. 'I'm going to make you comfortable and then we're going to get you out of here. Some of my colleagues are coming with a stretcher and we'll carry you back to the ambulance. What's your name?'

'Verity. Verity Williams. This is so embarrassing.' The woman closed her eyes briefly. 'I've always scoffed at people who need the services of the mountain rescue team—always thought they were frivolous or badly equipped.'

Miranda shot a guilty look at Jake, who winked at her.

'It can happen to the best of us, Verity. Now, if you don't mind, I'm just going to take a look at the damage.' His tone reassuring, he undid the laces of her boot and Miranda caught hold of the woman's hand and encouraged her to squeeze.

'Oh, that's agony!' Verity's face drained of colour and she gasped in pain as Jake carefully eased the boot off her foot.

Miranda pulled a face. She could see instantly that Verity's foot was badly swollen and discoloured. Was it broken? And what, she wondered, was Jake going to do about that out here in the middle of nowhere?

'Does it hurt here?' Jake was examining the ankle carefully and the woman gasped again.

'Yes. It's just a sprain, I'm sure, not a break.' She winced and tried to wriggle into a more comfortable position while Jake dug his mobile phone out of his pocket and opened the top of his rucksack.

He pulled out a pad, a coiled rope and a knife and set about making a splint, his movements slick and confident.

'Miranda, can you just check her pedal pulse? The foot looks a reasonable colour and she has sensation and movement so I'm assuming her circulation isn't impaired, but I want to check.' The phone tucked under his ear, he started talking to the person on the other end, giving a report on the woman's condition and a description of their whereabouts, while he cut the pad and fashioned a splint.

Miranda removed her glove and checked the pulse in the woman's foot, feeling the delicate throb under her fingertips with relief. 'She has a good pulse,' she told Jake as he snapped the phone shut and finished splinting the leg.

'Right.' Jake secured the splint and glanced at his watch. 'I think they'll be along with that stretcher in another fifteen minutes, Verity, so hang in there.'

'Fifteen minutes?' Miranda gaped at him. 'It's taken us almost an hour to get to this point.'

'The mountain rescue team aren't in the advanced stages of pregnancy,' he reminded her, rocking back on his heels and pushing his hand back into his rucksack.

Verity's face brightened. 'You're about to have a baby? Oh, you lucky things. How wonderful for you.'

Miranda frowned. 'Well, actually, the baby isn't—'

'We're thrilled,' Jake said firmly, pulling out an extra layer and slipping it around Verity's shoulders. 'Best thing that could have happened.'

Confused as to why he would let the woman continue with her misunderstanding, Miranda opened her mouth to correct him and gave a gasp of shock as Jake leaned forward and kissed her. 'I'm plucking up courage to ask her to marry me,' he murmured, 'but I have a feeling she's going to turn me down so I keep postponing the moment.'

Marry him?

Miranda was speechless and Verity gave a sigh.

'You don't want to marry him?' She turned to look at Miranda who managed a weak smile.

'I haven't known him that long.' Realising how that sounded, Miranda felt a rush of embarrassment. What would Verity think of her? *She could hardly explain that she couldn't marry him because she was pregnant with another man's baby, could she?*

'I knew my husband for about five minutes before I realised that he was the one.' Verity sighed. 'When it's right, there's just no point in waiting.'

Jake smiled. 'My point exactly.'

Miranda looked at him, trying to read his mind. Was he serious? Why did something that seemed so complicated to her seem so simple to everyone else?

Still reeling from his words, she tried to concentrate as Jake engaged Verity in conversation about marriage, babies and life generally, but her mind kept wandering back to his surprise announcement.

Did he really want to marry her?

And then she glanced across at him, saw the way he was taking Verity's mind off the pain with an animated discussion on the risks of a certain climbing technique and she suddenly realised that he'd just been trying to distract Verity.

Her spirits slumped and she gave an irritated frown, totally unable to understand her own reaction. She didn't want to marry him. She didn't want to marry anyone. So why did the realisation that his proposal had been nothing more than distraction therapy leave her feeling so flat?

'Here come the cavalry.' Rising to his feet in an athletic movement, Jake gave Verity a quick smile. 'We'll soon have you back to civilisation.'

'What a pity.' Verity glanced round her with a sigh. 'I love it here. This view is vastly preferably to the view from my office window, but there you are. Can't always have what you want in life.'

'Why not? I always think that what you want is worth fighting for.' Jake's gaze lingered on Miranda for a brief moment and then he turned his attention to his colleagues who arrived carrying the stretcher and other equipment.

After that it all happened so quickly and smoothly that Miranda could do little except watch in amazement.

With the efficiency of a team clearly used to working together, they assembled the stretcher and in no time at all they were ready to carry her Verity along the path towards the ambulance.

'I'm not going to be able to keep up with you,' Miranda told Verity, 'so I'll say goodbye now. I hope your ankle doesn't take long to heal.'

'And I hope you agree to marry your young man!' Verity smiled her thanks at Jake. 'Men like him don't come along very often. You should snap him up.'

'I agree. She definitely should.' Ignoring the curious glances of the rest of the team, Jake strolled back to collect his gear, leaving his colleagues to set off down the path.

Miranda stood still, chewing her lip, a frown on her face. 'Don't you mind that they're all gossiping now?'

'Why would I mind?'

'You let her think that the baby is yours and that you want to marry me. Just how far are you prepared to go in the name of distraction?'

'It wasn't about distraction.' He swung his rucksack onto his back. 'I'm crazy about you, Miranda, and the baby is part of you. You've got to stop thinking that your pregnancy makes any difference to the way I feel about you.'

The way he felt about her?

She felt suddenly light-headed. *He was crazy about her?* She felt a flicker of happiness and excitement that she ruthlessly squashed. 'You might think you don't mind about the baby, but that's before reality sets in.'

His eyes were amused. 'You think I don't know about babies?'

'You know about *delivering* babies, Jake. Delivering them isn't the same as living with them.' Especially when that baby wasn't his.

'I have nieces and nephews. I'm a very hands-on uncle and godfather.'

'And you return home to your perfect, peaceful house at night. It isn't the same thing at all!'

He took her arm and tucked it through his as they walked back down the path towards the car. 'I'm not precious about my house, Miranda. A house is a home, not a showpiece, despite what my sister may think.'

'Do you have any idea what children would do to your cream sofa?'

'Actually, yes,' he said in a lazy, masculine drawl. 'My godson, Ben, is always spilling drinks. My sofa has been the lucky recipient on at least three occasions.'

She sighed. 'You've got an answer for everything.'

'If you're telling me that I'm persistent, yes, I am. But I'm also patient.' The amusement in his eyes faded. 'I don't want you to feel under pressure. I'm willing to wait for you to make the first move.'

They were back at the car and she'd never felt so confused in her life. 'I'm not going to make the first move.'

He unlocked the car with a smile, his expression unperturbed. 'Then we're in for a frustrating few months, angel. Good job there are plenty of frozen lakes for me to jump into.'

* * *

He kept his word about not making the first move and for the next two weeks they worked together, ate dinner together, chatted about everything. But he didn't kiss her. And she didn't kiss him.

What was the point, when she knew it wasn't going anywhere?

No matter how great the attraction, she wasn't willing to subject herself to more trauma when it ended, and she knew it would end.

So she gritted her teeth and ignored the rush of excitement she felt whenever he walked into a room and she forced herself not to stare at him when they ate a meal together and not once did she reach for him even though her hands were burning to touch him.

Jake himself worked punishing hours, sometimes spending whole nights at the hospital, returning home briefly just to shower and shave before returning to do his ward round. His commitment to his patients was absolute and his skill and patience with the mothers astonished her. And she learned a great deal from him and found her confidence growing. He taught her to trust her instincts and not doubt herself.

Just how far she'd come was brought home to her when a young woman was admitted to the labour ward with flu-like symptoms.

Miranda helped her into one of the side rooms and quickly glanced at the letter from the GP. Clearly he'd spoken to one of the obstetric registrars, who had then arranged for admission.

'I've never had a headache like this,' the woman groaned softly as she curled up on the bed and covered her face with her arms. 'I feel totally hideous—you have no idea.'

'I'm going to phone the doctor to tell him you're here and then I'm going to make you more comfortable,' Miranda told her gently, frowning slightly as she touched the woman's forehead. She was burning hot and the expression in her eyes was slightly glazed.

Feeling very uneasy and unwilling to leave the woman on her own, Miranda was about to hit the buzzer when Jake's SHO, Belinda Morris, walked into the room.

'Hi, there. I spoke to the GP about Cathy,' she said cheerfully, walking over to the bed and giving the woman a sympathetic look. 'I'm Dr Morris. You poor thing. Flu is rotten at any time, but even more so when you're pregnant. Life can be very unfair.'

Clearly the junior doctor wasn't in the least alarmed by Cathy's condition and Miranda forced herself to relax, telling herself that she was just being hypersensitive. It was just because of that one case of shoulder dystocia, she told herself. She'd been imagining emergencies with every patient since then.

While Dr Morris carried out an examination, Miranda checked Cathy's temperature and found it to be extremely high.

'No surprises there, then,' Dr Morris said briskly, when Miranda showed her the reading.

Still telling herself that she was being over-anxious, Miranda slipped off Cathy's top and frowned. 'How long have you had this rash, Cathy?'

Cathy lay with her eyes closed. Her breathing was shallow and her cheeks were flushed. 'Don't know,' she murmured finally. 'Nothing there this morning.'

'Viral rashes are very common with flu,' Belinda said briskly, pushing her stethoscope back in her pocket. 'They resolve over time. Nothing to worry about.'

Miranda wished she felt equally confident. Suddenly her anxiety refused to be suppressed. 'I think we should call Mr Blackwell.'

'He's in a meeting at the moment. We'll just keep her in for the time being, monitor the baby and see how she goes.'

Belinda walked towards the door with a confident and slightly superior smile. 'I'll let Jake know that she's here. Call me if anything changes.'

The door closed behind her and Miranda looked at the rash again. Viruses often cause a rash, she repeated to herself. Viruses often cause a rash. On impulse she picked up a glass from the side of the bed and pressed it against the woman's skin. The rash didn't blanch.

Without hesitation, Miranda hit the emergency button and seconds later Ruth came running in.

Her anxiety levels soaring, Miranda checked Cathy's temperature again, her hands shaking slightly. 'Call Mr Blackwell. Call him now.' She hesitated briefly. 'And we need to give her intravenous penicillin right away.'

Ruth looked at her and then the rash. 'Right. I'll arrange it.' Without argument or discussion, she left the room and was back moments later accompanied by Jake.

Miranda had never been so relieved to see anyone. Calmed by his presence, she turned back to her patient. 'When did you start to feel ill, Cathy?'

'Last night.' Cathy moved her arms and opened her eyes. 'I can see two of you,' she murmured drowsily. 'Is that normal?'

Jake strode over to the bedside. He was dressed in a beautifully cut suit that emphasised the width of his shoulders and the strength of his physique. He looked serious and businesslike and the usual humour was missing from his blue eyes. It was obvious that he'd come straight from a difficult meeting and Miranda felt a flash of insecurity.

What if she'd bothered him for no reason? What if she was wrong?

She came straight to the point. 'Cathy was sent in by her GP with flu-like symptoms but she has a rash on her torso and I think we should probably give her penicillin right away.' She didn't want to mention the word 'meningitis' because she didn't want to frighten the patient and she didn't want to waste time taking Jake out of the room to brief him on her fears.

Jake took one look at Cathy and reached into his pocket for a tourniquet. 'Have you got the penicillin there?' His voice calm, he held out a hand for the syringe which Ruth handed him and quickly checked the ampoule. 'Great. We're just going to give you an injection of some antibiotic, Cathy, and then we're going to take some blood and get you transferred somewhere more comfortable. Are you allergic to penicillin?'

Eyes closed, Cathy shook her head slowly and Jake injected the penicillin just as Belinda came back into the room.

'Oh, Jake, I didn't know you were out of your meeting. I was going to tell you about Cathy when you—'

'I want you to take blood cultures and then start an infusion.' Discarding the empty syringe, Jake rose to his feet, his handsome face serious. 'I'm going to talk to ITU.'

'ITU?' Belinda frowned. 'But I—'

'Cultures.' Jake's tone was cool. 'Ruth—get me Geoff Masters on the phone, please. He's the consultant in Communicable Disease Control. I need to tell him what's happening.'

After that things moved swiftly. Cathy was transferred to ITU and Jake continued to liaise with other consultants over her management.

'He's been up on ITU for hours,' Ruth told Miranda later as they changed to go home. 'No one has ever seen a case of meningitis in a pregnant woman before so they're all huddled around, discussing the best way to treat her.'

'Is she worse?'

'No. Better, apparently. Thanks to the brilliance of a certain midwife on the labour ward—Jake's words, by the way, not mine.' Ruth wriggled into a thick jumper and reached for her coat. 'He hauled Dr Morris over the coals. Wanted to know why she hadn't called him the second she set eyes on the patient.'

Miranda grabbed her bag out of her locker. 'Maybe she was afraid of getting him out of a meeting.'

Ruth gave her a pointed look. 'You weren't.'

'I think that case of shoulder dystocia has made me jumpy. I see emergencies everywhere.'

'Well, that's fortunate for young Cathy, then, but I think you're dismissing what you've done rather lightly. Jake is asking questions as to why the GP didn't give her penicillin.'

'Well, to be fair, meningitis wouldn't be the first thing you think of in a pregnant woman with a temperature and a rash,' Miranda murmured, and Ruth stopped and looked at her.

'You thought of it.'

'And thank goodness for that.' Jake's deep drawl came from the doorway and both Ruth and Miranda turned in surprise.

'You're not supposed to come in here,' Ruth scolded. 'This is the midwives' changing room. It could be full of naked women.'

Jake smiled placidly. 'I keep hoping.'

'How is she?'

'Better.' Jake's blue eyes were warm as he turned to look at Miranda. 'And it's undoubtedly thanks to you. If you hadn't insisted on calling me and having the penicillin ready, it might have been a different story.'

'I was afraid I might be wasting your time.'

'I suspect you might have just saved two lives so any time you feel the inclination to bother me, please, do so.'

'I'm just so relieved she's all right.'

'Well, she's not totally out of the woods, but she's definitely responding to antibiotics and all the scans and blood tests suggest that the baby is all right, although we won't know for sure until it's delivered.'

Ruth put her coat on. 'If it's been confirmed as meningitis, shouldn't Miranda take Rifampicin or something?'

Jake shook his head. 'We've talked about that. For healthcare professionals it's really only recommended if you've given mouth-to-mouth or similar. Given Miranda is pregnant, I'd be reluctant to give her anything, and Geoff Masters agrees.'

'I wasn't with her for that long,' Miranda said reasonably. 'She was transferred almost immediately. All I really did was take her temperature.'

Jake nodded. 'The risk is minuscule.' He glanced at his watch. 'I've told them to call me if there's any change. Let's go home.'

Aware that Ruth was looking at her with a quizzical expression on her face, Miranda sighed. 'Jake's very generously letting me a room in his house, just until I find somewhere suitable.'

'Good.' Ruth beamed at both of them, swept up her bag and walked towards the door. 'I'm off, then. Need to feed my husband and recharge my batteries, ready for another exciting day in the office tomorrow. I feel we're in desperate need of a run of normal deliveries, just so that we can all remind ourselves that sometimes it can all go swimmingly well, without any of this drama and tension.'

Miranda and Jake walked towards the car. 'You must be knackered.' He unlocked the car door and held it open while she slid inside.

'I am tired.'

'Quick supper and early bed.' He drove home quickly, a slight frown on his face as he concentrated on the road.

Sneaking a glance at his strong profile, Miranda wondered what he was thinking. Was he worrying about Cathy?

'What on earth made you even think of meningitis? It obviously didn't cross the minds of the GP or my SHO.'

'I've seen a similar rash before. In a child when I was doing a paediatric module.'

'Lucky for Cathy.' He turned the car into his drive and pulled up outside the house. 'You go and have a bath. I'll knock something up for supper.'

'I'm cooking tonight.' Miranda undid her seat belt and wriggled out of the car. Her bump was starting to feel larger by the day.

'No way.'

'Jake, you don't have to wait on me. I want to cook. It's my turn. Why don't you have a bath? By the time you've finished, I'll have it ready.'

He opened his mouth to argue and then clearly saw something in her eyes that made him change his mind because he smiled. 'Good. Fine. In that case, I'll go for a quick run. I haven't done any exercise for days. It clears my head and removes the stress.'

'There's snow on the ground.'

'It muffles the sound of my bones creaking,' he drawled, humour gleaming in his blue eyes. 'Short run, quick shower then supper. All right with you?'

Miranda took a quick shower herself and changed then wandered into the beautiful, spacious kitchen.

She ran a hand over the smooth work surface, her expression wistful. Who could dislike cooking in surroundings like these?

Pulling herself together, she opened the fridge, pulled out some chicken and vegetables and started chopping.

By the time Jake came back from his run she had garlic and ginger sizzling in a pan and all the ingredients prepared.

'Smells delicious. ' He sniffed the contents of the pan and smiled. 'Stir-fry?'

'Is that all right with you? It's just that it's quick and—'

'It's perfect. I'll be back down in three minutes if I skip a shave.'

She tossed chicken in the hot oil, added water to the noodles and was just assembling everything when he appeared in the doorway, dark hair still damp from the shower. Her heart lurched and her insides shifted alarmingly. Suddenly she wished he'd taken the extra few minutes to shave. Why did the stubble make him more attractive? Was it because he looked less like a respectable consultant and more...dangerous?

She permitted herself a wry smile. All men were dangerous. She knew that better than anyone. Giving herself a sharp talking-to, she rescued the plates that she had warming in the oven and lifted the pan from the heat.

'Sit down, it's ready.'

'I have to confess that I love it when you cook.' He leaned forward and gave an appreciative sniff. 'You're very creative in the kitchen.'

'I love your kitchen.' She served a generous portion onto his plate and then took a smaller helping herself. 'What about you?'

'I don't think it's one of my more obvious talents, but I manage.'

'Did your mother teach you the basics?'

'Are you joking?' He picked up his fork with a grin. 'My mother doesn't let anyone into her kitchen. My sister took pity on me after spending a weekend. Or, I suppose, if I'm honest, she took pity on herself. She was fed up with eating my idea of food. How did you learn? Did your mother teach you to cook?'

Her hand froze on the fork. It was a perfectly reasonable question. Hadn't she just asked him exactly the same one? 'No.' She couldn't keep the stiffness out of her tone. 'No, she didn't. I taught myself.'

His gaze lingered on her face for a moment and then he turned his attention back to his plate. 'You've always said that you don't have any family. What happened?'

She put her fork down, her appetite suddenly gone. 'I suppose I do have family.' She almost choked on the word and wondered why she didn't just lie. 'It's just that we're not in touch any more.'

'And you don't want to talk about it.' His tone was gentle, his blue eyes suddenly intent as he studied the tension in her face. 'All right, we'll talk about something else. Are you sleeping better now?'

She gave a faint smile. 'Hard not to in that amazing bed.'

'Another one of my sister's purchases. She always said that since she was my most frequent guest, she was going to buy herself a comfortable bed to sleep in.'

'You mentioned a niece and nephews, so she's obviously married.'

'Oh, yes. To an architect. They worked together on a project, that's how they met.' Jake leaned forward and helped himself to more food. 'And now I have two cheeky nephews and a baby niece.'

Envy sliced through her and she gave a puzzled frown. Why envy? She never envied families. She knew that they were rarely what they seemed. 'Do they live far away?'

'Far enough.' He leaned forward, picked up her fork and handed it to her. 'Eat, or I'll have to force-feed you.'

'I'm not that hungry.'

'Eat.'

Feeling thoroughly unsettled and not really understanding why, Miranda speared a thin strip of chicken and nibbled it. 'Why do you say far enough? You're obviously close to her.'

'We're twins,' Jake confessed. 'So, yes, we're close. A bit too close sometimes. She's inclined to meddle in my life.'

'Like decorating your house?'

'That sort of meddling I can live with.' He picked up his glass. 'What I don't like is her interference in my love life. She's always inviting me to dinner and introducing me to yet another of her recently divorced, unattached friends.'

Miranda couldn't help smiling. 'It's pretty hard to meet people. That sounds as good a way as any.'

'That's because you don't know my sister.' Jake suppressed a yawn and pushed his chair away from the table. 'Let's just say that her idea of my ideal woman and my idea of my ideal woman don't exactly coincide.'

'What's your ideal woman?' The moment she asked the question she wished she hadn't. His blue eyes lifted to hers and didn't shift.

'I'm looking at her.'

She gave a soft gasp and looked away. 'Jake...'

'I know what you're going to say next so I'll save you the breath and that way you can concentrate on clearing the food on your plate. You're going to say that I've only known you a short time, you're going to remind me that you're pregnant, just in case I'd forgotten, and then you're going to say that you're not interested in men because relationships always go wrong.'

It was so close to what she would have said that she gaped at him. 'Are you a mind-reader?'

'No, but I think I probably understand women better than most men.' He put his glass down on the table and leaned forward, his eyes still on her face. 'I have a twin sister and on top of that I spend every day talking to women at a time when they're at their most emotionally vulnerable. I have a pretty good idea what all your arguments will be, although I don't understand all your reasons because you don't trust me enough to tell me about your family. I'm hoping that, in time, that will change.'

She stared at him, stunned by what he was saying. 'I've told you about Peter.'

'Yes. But there's more and that's fine.' His tone was conversational, as if they were discussing nothing more serious than the weather. 'I'm willing to wait until you're ready to tell me.'

She was his ideal woman?

'Jake—'

'I'm not expecting a response to what I just said.' He stood up and flicked on the kettle. 'You asked me about my ideal woman and I told you.'

'But that's ridiculous.' Her voice was hoarse. 'Why would you be interested in me? What could I possibly have that you want?'

He turned to face her, dark lashes partially shielding the expression in his eyes. 'You don't have a very high opinion of yourself, do you, sweetheart?'

'I just don't see why a man like you would be interested in a woman like me. It doesn't make sense.'

'A man like me?' He raised an eyebrow in question. 'What sort of woman should a man like me be interested in, Miranda? Tell me. I'm intrigued to know.'

She took a deep breath. 'You're clever and good-looking, you don't need me to tell you that. You must have hopeful women trailing after you in droves. You certainly don't need someone as—' She broke off and hesitated. 'Complicated. You don't need someone as complicated as me.'

'You've worked with me for long enough to know that I thrive on complicated. I find routine and predictability unspeakably boring.' He smiled. 'Finish your dinner, Miranda, and stop worrying.'

She ignored her food. 'I need you to know that nothing is going to happen between us. Not ever. I just don't—'

'It's already happened and you know it.' His voice level, he spooned coffee into a cafetiere and picked up the kettle. 'There's a connection between us that we cannot possibly deny, but I understand that this is a big thing for you. So we'll just live with it for a bit and see where our relationship goes. I'm a patient man.'

'Patience has nothing to do with it and our relationship isn't going anywhere!' There was a note of panic in her voice. Why wasn't he listening to her? 'And what do you mean, it's a big thing for me? Given that you're in your thirties and single, it would seem a reasonable guess that a relationship is a big thing for you, too.'

With a sigh he leaned forward and removed the redundant fork from her numb fingers. 'It's big, yes. Of course it is. But I'm not scared of commitment. And I'm only single because I'm very, very choosy.'

'Have you ever been in love?' The question flew from her lips before she could stop it, and he paused for a moment.

'Yes.' His voice was quiet. 'Once.'

'What happened?'

His hesitation was fractional. 'Before I could say anything to her, she fell in love with another man. Chances are it wouldn't have made a difference if I'd spoken up earlier, but I made a promise to myself that if I ever met another woman who affected me as much as she did, I was going to tell her straight away.' He stabbed some food onto the fork and held it to her mouth. 'Eat, sweetheart. The baby needs it even if you don't.'

Why did the moment seem so impossibly intimate? The words he'd just spoken? Or the look in his sexy blue eyes or the fact that he was feeding her with her own fork? Whichever, she felt warm colour touch her cheekbones.

If he was choosy, why had he chosen her when she surely possessed none of the attributes that he was likely to look for in a prospective partner? She wanted to ask about the other woman. The woman he'd been in love with. But she was all too aware that she was probing into his life while revealing nothing about her own.

Why did she want to know about him?

Why was she interested?

Confused and unsettled, she took the fork from his hand and finished the food on her plate, knowing that he was right that she needed to eat. The fact that she didn't feel hungry was irrelevant.

It didn't matter that he was patient, she told herself as she chewed listlessly. And it didn't matter that he thrived on complications. It didn't even matter that he'd been honest and told her how he felt. Their relationship wasn't going anywhere. All right, so there was chemistry there, she'd be a fool to deny it. But chemistry didn't make a firm foundation for a relationship. Nothing did.

There was no way she'd risk ever exposing her child to a relationship that would inevitably go wrong.

Not even with a man as seductively attractive as Jake Blackwell.

CHAPTER EIGHT

WHY did he always fall in love with unobtainable women?

Working his way through a busy antenatal clinic the next morning, Jake found his attention wandering back to the previous evening.

Of all the women he'd ever met, he'd never encountered one as complex and wary as Miranda. How could a woman be both spirited and fiercely independent and yet touchingly vulnerable at the same time? What had happened in her past to score such deep wounds through her confidence? What had created that determined independence? Genetic make-up or the influence of family?

There was obviously something in her past, something that she refused to reveal. It was impossible to move forward, to counter her fears and anxieties, when he didn't understand the cause. He was determined to find out more about her. Determined to give her the confidence to open up and confide in him.

Patience, he reminded himself as he checked a set of blood results that one of the midwives had handed him. Patience. Hopefully, given time, she'd be able to trust him. In the meantime, he was going to make sure that they spent as much time together as possible.

Given that they were working and living together, it proved gratifyingly easy.

He was called up to the labour ward later that afternoon to see Paula Webb, a woman who had been on the ward for two days following premature rupture of membranes.

'I started having contractions an hour ago. You said you thought that would happen. But I'm only thirty-five weeks, Mr Blackwell,' she muttered, and Jake gave her shoulder a squeeze.

'It's going to be fine, Paula. The baby's heart rate is doing exactly what we like it to do. Try not to worry. I've told you before, that's my job.'

'But it's too early.' Paula screwed up her face as another contraction took hold. 'Is he going to end up in an incubator?'

'I can't promise that he won't,' Jake said honestly, 'but in all likelihood he'll be fine.'

'I really want to have a normal delivery.'

'And that's exactly what we want.' Jake glanced at Miranda, who was looking after Paula. 'She's six centimetres now. There's no reason why she should have any problems but I'm around if you need me.'

Paula looked at him anxiously. 'What time are you going off duty?'

Jake smiled at her. 'When you've had your baby. I'll see you later.'

He walked out of the room and Paula gazed after him. 'He is such a lovely man. One of my friends had Mr Hardwick and she didn't see him once, not once in her entire pregnancy, but I've seen Mr Blackwell almost every time and now he says he won't even go home until I've had the baby.'

'He's an excellent obstetrician.' Miranda sat with Paula and monitored her contractions for the rest of the afternoon, and by five o'clock she was fully dilated and pushing.

Miranda hit the buzzer to ask for some help and then opened a delivery pack just as Ruth and Jake walked into the room.

'Everything all right here?' Jake glanced at the foetal heart rate and gave a satisfied nod. 'That looks good. How are you doing, Paula? Tired?'

'Determined.' Paula screwed up her face and pushed again. 'You're not going to use those forceps on me or do a Caesarean section.'

'Glad to hear it,' Jake's tone was mild. 'I'm essentially lazy by nature, so I have no intention of doing any of those things unless strictly necessary.'

'I can see the head, Paula,' Miranda said. 'One more push and I think we're there.'

Jake looked at Ruth. 'Call the paediatrician. Just in case.' He spoke softly so that Paula couldn't hear, and Miranda knew that he was still slightly concerned about the baby. He was a man who didn't take any chances and she liked that.

The paediatrician arrived just as the shoulder was delivered and the baby slithered into Miranda's waiting hands.

Immediately the baby howled with indignation and Miranda placed him gently in Paula's waiting arms.

'Your son, Paula,' she said huskily, and Paula's eyes filled with tears.

'Oh, he's so beautiful…' She turned her head against her husband's shoulder and he held her as she started to sob.

'I love you, Mike.'

'I love you, too, babe. We're a proper family now.' Her husband's voice was choked and Miranda swallowed down the lump in her throat.

What was the matter with her? She wasn't usually so emotional. It was impossible to watch Paula and her husband and not wonder what it must be like to have that sort of love and support from someone.

Fortunately the delivery was far from over and she concentrated on the placenta and then on making Paula comfortable, blocking out the emotional scenes in the delivery room.

She was still holding herself firmly in check when she walked to the car with Jake.

'That was such a nice delivery. I'm so glad it went smoothly for Paula.'

'Me, too.'

'They're a lovely family.'

'Yes.'

He glanced towards her. 'No cynical comment? Aren't you going to tell me that he's probably having an affair with someone else and she's really pleased because she hates him anyway?'

'No.' She interrupted him and looked away, unaware of the soft brush of snow on her cheeks. 'No, I'm not going to tell you that. I think Paula's lucky. I'm glad nothing went wrong. I was worried it might. You knew it would be all right, didn't you?'

He shrugged. 'No one can ever be certain, of course, but, yes, I had a good feeling.'

'How? Why?' She looked at him helplessly, wishing she had his antennae. 'You just seem to know when something is about to go wrong and you're always there to sort it out before things reach crisis point.'

He pressed the button on his keys and unlocked the doors. 'That's not instinct, that's experience.'

'But don't you ever panic?' She slid into the car and huddled her coat more closely around herself, suddenly feeling the cold. 'Things can go wrong in the blink of an eye in obstetrics but I've never seen you anything but calm.'

'Do I panic?' He started the engine and frowned thoughtfully. 'No. To be honest, I don't. I just see a problem and try and solve it.'

'You don't worry about the responsibility? Litigation?' Her teeth were chattering and she wished the car would warm up. 'These days everyone is trying to sue everyone.'

Jake laughed and reversed out of his parking space. 'Fortunately the UK isn't as bad as the US. In America they actually have groups of lawyers dedicated to suing us obstetricians for malpractice. Delightful.'

'How do you cope with the pressure?'

'I stay up to date, I listen to mothers and midwives, I don't ignore small warning signs because they invariably mean something and, having done all that, I relax. If you worry too much, you cease to be effective. Put my coat on. You're shivering.'

He noticed everything, she thought as she reached into the back seat for his coat and snuggled underneath it. 'Pregnant women are supposed to be hot all the time. I'm frozen.'

'Probably something to do with the fact that we had two inches of snow last night and you haven't eaten since lunchtime.' He turned the heat up in the car and took a sharp corner carefully, his hands steady on the wheel. 'You must be starving. Or, at least, I hope you are because you're about to be presented with a mountain of food.'

'We're going out?'

'I'm too tired to cook and I'm sick of pizza.' He suppressed a yawn. 'I'm taking you to dinner with some friends of mine. Christy is a wonderful cook. All we have to do is sit there and eat.'

She was horrified. 'But I can't just turn up to dinner! I don't know them and—'

'I know them.'

'But who are you going to say I am? How are you going to introduce me?'

He slowed the car as he drove down a narrow lane and

into a huge driveway. 'A friend? My lodger? How would you like me to introduce you?' He switched off the engine, gave her a maddeningly placid smile and then climbed out of the car.

She followed him with a million questions on her lips, none of which she was able to ask because instantly the door opened and a beautiful red-headed woman stood there, smiling.

'I hope you're hungry because I've over-catered.'

'Those are the words I've been fantasising about all day. No lunch—big appetite. Hello, my angel, how are you?' Jake leaned forward and kissed the woman warmly. Miranda stopped dead, suddenly feeling all sorts of things that she didn't want to feel.

Who was the red-headed woman?

And why did she feel such a powerful urge to know?

Jake was perfectly entitled to have a girlfriend.

She was still trying to rationalise her thoughts when a handsome, dark-haired man appeared behind the woman. 'Unhand my wife, Blackwell.'

His wife?

The tension left Miranda and she had a wonderful evening. The conversation was lively and the food excellent. After tucking into salmon in a creamy herb sauce, Miranda helped clear the plates and was immediately trapped by Christy in the kitchen.

'So—where did you meet Jake?'

Miranda put the plates down on the table. 'We're working together,' she said carefully, deciding not to reveal the story of their Christmas Day meeting.

'That's nice.'

'I'm just his lodger. We're friends, nothing more,' Miranda said hastily, and Christy shot her a searching look as she pulled open the fridge door and removed a large fruit salad.

'Am I allowed to ask about the baby or is it a taboo subject?' Balancing the dish on one hand, Christy opened a drawer and rummaged for a large spoon with the other. 'If it's a tactless question, ignore me.'

'It's not tactless.' Miranda rubbed a hand over her abdomen. 'I'm seven months pregnant but I'm not with the father any more. It was a short relationship and he turned out to be married. I didn't know that until afterwards.' Somehow it was important to her that Christy knew the truth.

'Ouch. You poor thing.' Christy's voice was soft. 'That must be difficult for you. Still, at least you have Jake now.'

'Oh, no!' Miranda looked at her, startled. 'I don't have Jake. It isn't like that at all. He just—'

'He just can't take his eyes off you,' Christy finished with a womanly smile. 'I've never seen Jake so smitten and I've known him for a long time. I'm thrilled. Alessandro and I have been waiting for him to meet someone special.'

'I'm just his lodger.'

Christy's smile widened. 'To the best of my knowledge, Jake doesn't have any financial problems, so his reasons for wanting you to share his house must amount to more than a boost to his income.'

'He's been very kind to me, that's true, but—'

'You're the first woman he's ever brought to dinner here so that says a lot.' Juggling fruit salad and bowls, Christy walked back towards the kitchen door where she paused. 'Jake's had plenty of girlfriends but hardly any serious relationships. I just want you to know that. Be kind to him.'

Be kind to him?

And suddenly, without a shadow of a doubt, Miranda knew that Christy was the woman Jake had been in love with.

When? He didn't seem like the type to chase after a married woman.

Her own mind suddenly full of questions, she followed Christy back to the table and Jake looked up.

'You were a long time. Everything OK?'

'Fine.' Miranda managed a smile and Christy dished out fruit salad.

'My fault. I was delving into all her secrets. Woman's prerogative.'

Jake's gaze was thoughtful but he didn't pursue the subject until they were safely back in the car.

'I'm sorry if Christy upset you. It didn't occur to me that she'd ask you questions about your pregnancy, but perhaps it was inevitable.'

'She didn't upset me. She's really nice.'

'And Alessandro?'

Miranda thought about the dark-haired, brooding A and E consultant who had challenged his wife on so many points. 'A bit intimidating,' she said honestly.

'Most women find him irresistible.' Jake's tone was dry. 'Mediterranean heritage and all that.'

'She was the one, wasn't she?' Miranda couldn't not ask the question. 'Christy was the woman you were in love with.'

'What makes you say that?'

'Just something she said when we were in the kitchen. Something about her caring about you.' She frowned slightly and Jake gave a smile.

'I should hope that she does care about me. That's what friends are supposed to do and, yes, Christy is the woman I was in love with, but it was a long time ago.'

'Does she know?'

'Yes.' Jake's voice was calm. 'Funnily enough, I told her just before Christmas.'

'This Christmas?'

'That's right. She and Alessandro were going through a bad

patch. I wanted to remind her that what they had was special. Worth fighting for. I gave her up because I could see that they were perfect together. They still are.'

'You really believe in perfection? Isn't that rather romantic and idealistic? If you expect perfection then any relationship is doomed to fall apart.'

'I didn't say I believed in perfection, I said that they were perfect together. *Not* the same thing. In fact, I would say that it's their imperfections that make them so perfect.'

Miranda laughed. 'Now you've lost me.'

'Well, they both have fiery tempers and they tend to communicate by flinging plates at each other and a great deal of hand-waving and raised voices. Hardly perfect. But they understand each other. They love each other. It works for them.'

She stared at him. 'Ever considered being a marriage guidance counsellor?'

'No. Far too depressing. A large number of people who marry do so for all the wrong reasons. Those marriages cannot possibly be saved and then they're faced with all sorts of nasty, uncomfortable decisions, like whether they should stay together for the sake of the children, that sort of thing.'

'Why did Christy and Alessandro separate?'

Jake was silent for a moment. 'They didn't really. It was a classic case of miscommunication. I suppose they lost their way for a while. It happens all too easily. It's why it's so important to share things with your partner.' He glanced towards her. 'What do you think makes a relationship work?'

'I don't know many relationships that *have* worked so I'm not a good person to ask.' She looked out of the window and recognised the road. 'Oh—we're very near to my old flat. Can we just stop for a second so that I can drop my spare set of keys with the landlord?'

'Can't we just post them?'

'It will only take a minute—I'll just pop them through his letter-box.'

Jake took the necessary detour and pulled up outside the unwelcoming block of flats. 'Give me the keys—I'll do it. I don't want you anywhere near that place.'

'We'll go together. Look what happened last time you went on your own.' Miranda undid her seat belt. 'Someone needs to keep an eye on you. If he happens to be there, I don't want him hitting you again.'

His eyes gleamed with humour. 'What are you, my bodyguard?'

'Absolutely. Pregnant bodyguards are all the rage, haven't you heard?'

As it turned out, the landlord's flat was in darkness and they posted the keys through the door without mishap. They were just returning to the car when Miranda stopped dead.

'What was that?'

'What was what?' Jake gave a shiver and pulled his coat around him. 'It's freezing, Miranda. Get in the car, quickly.'

Miranda frowned and glanced around her. 'I heard something—a weird sound. I'm not sure what it was.'

'Probably the sound of my teeth chattering.' Jake grabbed her arm and tried to guide her towards the car but she shrugged him off.

'Wait. Listen…' She strained her ears and thought she heard a faint mewing sound. 'There. I heard it again.'

'Me, too—a cat, definitely a cat.'

Unconvinced, she turned in the direction of the sound. 'I don't know. It didn't sound much like a cat.'

'Miranda, for goodness' sake, it must be below freezing tonight and you're—'

'Wait there just for a minute.' Without giving him time to argue, she hurried back towards the building and into the stairwell. Lying on the ground was a pile of abandoned plastic shopping bags. There was no sign of a cat.

Miranda glanced around her, searching for the animal that had made the noise, but there was nothing. No sound and no movement. Presuming that whatever creature had made the noise had now found refuge somewhere warm, she turned to walk back to Jake when she heard the sound again.

This time there was no mistaking the sound and she ran back towards the plastic bags with a cry of horror. 'Oh, no! Jake—come quickly.'

'Miranda, I've told you that we need to—' He broke off as he saw what she was holding. 'Oh, my God.' His voice hoarse with disbelief, he dropped to his knees beside her. 'Is she breathing?'

Choked with horror, Miranda cuddled the tiny baby against her. 'Yes, but she's blue with cold. Oh, Jake, someone's just left her here.'

'And quite recently, too, by the looks of it.' Jake's expression was grim as he glanced around them. 'She can't be more than a few minutes old.'

'We need to look for the mother.'

'We need to get that baby to hospital,' Jake said immediately, standing up and punching a series of numbers into his mobile phone. 'Put her inside your clothes, Miranda, next to your skin. Then go and sit in my car. I'll turn the heater up.'

Her hands shaking, Miranda did as he instructed, tucking the tiny baby against her chest and then closing her cardigan and her coat around her. 'She's freezing, Jake.'

'I've rung Special Care—they'll have a cot ready if we take her straight there.'

Miranda glanced back over her shoulder towards the darkness of the stairwell. 'But the mother—'

'The baby has to be the priority. Once she's safely in the

hands of the paediatricians, we'll worry about the mother.' Jake slid the car into gear and drove quickly but carefully towards the hospital.

In no time at all the baby was in an incubator, surrounded by skilled staff all assessing her condition and speculating on her identity.

Miranda and Jake retreated to the tiny staffroom and were in the process of warming themselves up with hot coffee when the police arrived to take statements.

Jake spoke to them and then the consultant paediatrician walked into the room. 'She's very cold and dehydrated. It's a miracle you found her when you did. Any longer and she would have died of hypothermia without any doubt at all.'

The policeman frowned. 'She wasn't wrapped up at all?'

Miranda shook her head. 'Just inside plastic bags.'

'On a night like this?' The man's mouth tightened with disapproval. 'What must the mother have been thinking?'

Miranda put her coffee down on the table. 'I don't suppose she was thinking at all,' she said quietly, her voice shaking slightly. 'I expect she was too busy panicking.'

'Miranda's right.' Jake rubbed a hand over the back of his neck, his eyes tired. 'Whoever the mother is, she was obviously terrified and completely alone. I'm guessing that we're talking about a teenager and she needs help, possibly urgently. We must try and find her.'

The policeman blinked and then cleared his throat. 'Of course, yes. You're right. We'll arrange for house-to-house enquiries and we'll contact the news stations and broadcast an appeal.'

The paediatrician looked at Miranda. 'The nurses wondered if you wanted to give her a name.'

'Me?'

'Yes. You found her.'

'Oh…' Miranda thought for a moment and then gave a faint smile. 'Bonnie. She's such a pretty little thing.'

'Bonnie, it is.' The policeman scribbled on his pad. 'I'll be in touch. If there's any change in the baby, give us a call.'

He left the room and Miranda turned to Jake, her expression urgent.

'We have to try and find her. The mother, I mean.'

His eyes met hers. 'Miranda, the police are going to do house-to-house enquiries and—'

'And the police have absolutely no idea what it's like to be a terrified teenager.' She glanced towards the paediatrician. 'Bonnie's in good hands now. We can't do any more here.'

Jake's eyes slid to her abdomen. 'It's late, you're tired—'

'I couldn't possibly sleep knowing that a poor teenager is out there somewhere, terrified and possibly bleeding.' Her hands clenched into fists and Jake's eyes rested on her face.

'You don't know it's a teenager.'

She knew he was wondering why her reaction was so extreme but she didn't care. And she certainly didn't intend to offer an explanation. 'Jake!'

'All right.' He muttered something else under his breath and ran a hand through his hair. 'We'll go back to the flats and have a look around. But just for an hour. After that we're going home.'

Two police cars were parked outside the flats and Jake pulled up behind them while Miranda turned up her collar and wrapped her scarf round her neck.

'Do you have a torch?'

'Glove compartment.'

Miranda reached inside and tucked the torch in her pocket. 'Come on. Let's go.' She climbed out of the car and walked away from the flats, the beam of light from the torch flickering in front of her.

'Go where, exactly?' Fastening the buttons of his coat, Jake strode after her. 'Don't you think we should start by looking around the flats?'

'That's what the police are doing and I just don't think that's where she's going to be.'

'Why not? That was where she left the baby.'

'Because she wanted it to be found! But that doesn't mean that *she* wants to be found. Think about it, Jake! If she wanted her pregnancy to be made public then she would have turned up at an antenatal clinic. It's far more likely that she's avoiding people. Maybe she lives there, maybe her parents live there, but at the moment I think she's huddled in an alleyway somewhere, trying to work out what to do,' Miranda reasoned as she crossed the road and walked away from the flats. 'I don't believe she's in the flats.'

'You've missed your vocation.' Jake watched her with fascination as he kept pace. 'Have you been watching crime programmes in your spare time?'

'I don't have any spare time. I have work time and sleep time.' Miranda stopped dead, her frown slightly impatient as she tried to focus her mind. She looked around her, searching for inspiration, trying to think like a frightened teenager. 'What would you do, Jake? Think. You leave your baby somewhere where you know it's going to be found because you want it to be found.'

'Do you?' Jake scratched his head, trying to follow her train of thought. 'Miranda, perhaps we should leave this to the police. They have—'

'The park.' Miranda grabbed his arm and hurried along the road. 'I bet she's in the park.'

'This place has a park?' Jake glanced around him doubtfully and Miranda looked at him impatiently.

'It's where all the teenagers hang out. I've seen them.' She was half running now, her torch winking in the darkness. She pushed open the gate and paused.

Jake peered into the soupy darkness. 'She's not here.'

'You don't know that.' Miranda let the gate go and walked further into the park. 'This is just the play area for the little ones. Further in are bushes and trees. That's where the teenagers hang out. It's where they go to smoke.'

'How do you know all this?'

But before she could answer, Jake grabbed her arm. 'Over there.' He kept his voice low and pointed. 'To the right. Do you see it?'

Miranda followed the direction of his gaze and nodded. 'It's a person. Sitting on the ground. Oh, Jake, I'm sure that's her—'

'It might be nothing. Just a drunk. Miranda, you stay here and I'll go and see who it is.'

'No way. How is she going to react to being approached by a six-foot-two man she doesn't know?' Miranda shrugged him off and hurried across to the figure. 'Hello?' She swung the torch and the light suddenly illuminated a blotched, miserable face.

'G-go away.' The girl's voice was weak. 'I wanna be on my own.'

Miranda immediately dropped the torch and went down on her knees. 'I'm from the hospital. A midwife. We found a baby near here. Was it yours, sweetheart?'

Perhaps it was the endearment or just the relief of being found, but the girl started to sob quietly and the sound had a desperate quality that tore holes in Miranda's heart.

'Don't cry.' She slid her arms round the girl and held her. 'Please, don't cry. We're going to help you. I promise we'll help you.'

'I didn't know what was happening!' The girl choked and

sobbed, her words at times almost unintelligible as she talked. 'It hurt. It hurt so much and now the police are there.' The girl hiccoughed and wiped her nose on her sleeve. 'And I know the baby's dead and I'll go to prison. I killed her.'

'You won't go to prison. And she isn't dead. You haven't killed anyone.'

The girl was so distressed that she wasn't listening. 'She came out all blue and messy and I knew she was dead so I left her on the bags. I didn't know what else to do.'

'She isn't dead. Babies sometimes look a bit funny when they're born, that's all,' Miranda soothed, still holding the girl. 'She's beautiful and she's safely in hospital and that's exactly where you should go now. There are people there who will help you.'

Jake crouched down next to her and the girl shrank away, noticing him for the first time.

'Is he a cop?'

'No, he's a doctor. What's your name?'

The girl sniffed. 'Angie. Is the baby really OK?' Her voice was small and she sounded very, very young. 'I didn't want anything to happen to it. I was terrified when I thought it was dead.'

'She— The baby's a little girl. Angie,' Miranda's voice was gentle. 'Come to hospital with us now and we can make sure you're all right. Then someone will come and talk to you about the baby and you can decide what you want to do.'

'I can't keep her.' There was a note of panic in Angie's voice and Miranda hugged her.

'You're not in a fit state to make big decisions like that at the moment. You need help and I'm going to see that you get it. How old are you?'

'Sixteen.' Angie scrubbed at her face with the back of her hand. 'And I don't want to go to hospital. They'd tell my dad.'

'And would that be such a bad thing?'

'I dunno.' Angie sniffed again. 'I wanted to tell my mum but I was too scared. But now I just want to talk to her. I don't even care if she shouts at me. Will you ring her for me if I give you the number?'

'Let's get you to hospital,' Miranda said firmly, 'and once we know that you're fine, we'll help you with everything else.'

CHAPTER NINE

THE police were informed and Miranda stayed with Jake while he examined Angie and then waited until her parents arrived.

'Don't leave me,' Angie begged in a terrified voice, gripping Miranda's hand so tightly that she was given no choice in the matter. Not that she would have left.

Despite Jake's constant reminders that it was really late, that she was tired and should go home, she sat by Angie and talked to her, soothing and reassuring, unable to leave until she was sure that the young girl had someone with her who would care for her and offer the support she so badly needed.

The young teenager had calmed down and was sitting quietly when the door opened and a midwife came in, accompanied by Angie's mother.

Her hair was tangled and she'd obviously been woken from sleep and had dragged on the first clothes that came to hand. But there was no missing the worry in her eyes when she saw her daughter.

'Ange?'

Miranda felt a lump in her throat. What did the future hold for both of them? How would they manage? What would happen to Bonnie, currently lying in her cot, unaware that her whole future lay in the balance?

'Mum?' Angie's voice shook and she sounded like a very young girl. Nothing like the mother of a child. 'I'm really, really sorry…'

'I don't believe this! What have you been doing?' Her mother covered her mouth with her hand and Angie's face crumpled.

'I'm sorry,' she sobbed, 'I'm so, *so* sorry. Please, don't be angry. Please, don't yell. I didn't mean it to happen. I didn't know it would happen.' Her sobs were so pitiful that Miranda felt her own eyes fill with tears and she held the shaking girl, ready to defend her if necessary.

But it wasn't necessary.

Her mother crossed the room in a flash, tears pouring down her cheeks as she went to her daughter.

'There…' Her voice was choked. 'Don't cry, pet. Mummy's here and everything is going to be all right. We'll sort everything out. You should have told me. You should have told me, you silly thing.'

Angie sobbed and sobbed, her face blotched and swollen with crying. 'I didn't know how. I thought you'd be so mad with me. Dad's going to kill me.' She clung to her mother who shook her head slowly.

'Your dad's not going to kill anyone. He's just worried about you, love. We all are. I wish you'd told us. How did I not notice?' She glanced at Miranda with helpless confusion on her face, still visibly shocked by the circumstances. 'I thought she was putting on some weight so I've been encouraging her to eat a bit less, but it just never occurred to me…'

'You probably weren't looking for it,' Miranda said quietly, and the older woman gave a weary smile.

'Being a parent is the hardest thing in the world.' She stroked her daughter's hair with a gentle hand and instinctively Miranda knew what she was thinking. That her daughter was now a parent, too.

Angie sniffed. 'I don't know what to do, Mum.'

'What do you want to do, love? Whatever you choose, we'll support you.'

Miranda felt warmth and admiration spread through her. Lucky Angie, she thought to herself. Her mother wasn't trying to take over or dictate. She was trying to help her daughter make grown-up decisions by herself.

'I want to keep her.' Angie looked at her mother uncertainly. 'That's stupid, isn't it? I haven't even seen her yet but I know I want to keep her. When I thought she was dead I couldn't stop crying and now I know she's alive—'

'Why is it stupid?' Her mother straightened her shoulders. 'She's our flesh and blood. There'll be enough willing helpers, that's for sure. Of course we're going to keep her. She's family.'

It was two o'clock by the time Jake managed to persuade Miranda to leave, and he was worried by how drained and exhausted she looked.

'Are you all right? You haven't said a word since we left the hospital.' Knowing that she hadn't eaten since lunchtime, Jake made a mug of hot chocolate because he knew she loved it. 'Drink this and then go to bed. I've already agreed with Ruth that you're having tomorrow off. And just to make sure that you don't lift a finger, I'm having tomorrow off, too. After tonight's events, I think we both deserve it.'

'OK.' She didn't seem to be listening to him. And she didn't touch the hot chocolate—just stared into the mug and watched a skin form on the milk.

Deciding that sleep was the priority, he gently eased the mug from her hands and pulled her to her feet.

'You need to go to bed.' He led her up the stairs, opened

her bedroom door and gently nudged her inside. 'You did brilliantly with Angie, by the way. She's going to be all right now.'

'Is she? What about the baby?'

He frowned. 'The baby is doing well, Miranda. Thanks to the fact that you discovered her so quickly, she's going to be fine.'

'But what sort of life will she have?' Miranda turned to look at him and her dark eyes were huge and sad. 'Goodnight, Jake.' She closed the door, leaving him on the outside battling with a powerful inclination to go back inside and drag her into his arms.

He stared at the closed door, trying to work out what was going on in her mind.

What had she meant by that comment about the baby?

He ran a hand over the back of his neck, trying to decide what to do. She was tired, he reasoned, and pregnant women were always more emotional when they were tired.

The best thing was for her to have a good night's sleep.

They could talk in the morning.

He strolled into his bedroom and glanced at the clock with a humourless laugh. It was already morning.

He went to bed and woke suddenly to darkness and the sound of noises coming from the kitchen.

Miranda?

Tugging on his jeans, he padded downstairs.

She was sitting at the table with her head in her hands. Her dark hair flopped forward, hiding her face from his view, but he knew from the movement of her shoulders that she was crying. He swore softly under his breath and went straight to her, dragging out the chair next to her and sitting down.

'Miranda?' He put a hand on her shoulder and gave it a gentle shake. 'Sweetheart, what's wrong?'

For a long moment she didn't answer and then she lifted her head and the pain in her eyes shocked him.

'I just k-keep thinking about B-Bonnie.' She hiccoughed and he frowned slightly as he stroked her shoulders gently.

'Bonnie? But she's fine, angel. Doing really well. Thanks to you.'

Miranda shook her head and tears spilled down her cheeks. 'She's *not* fine. She has a mother too young to look after her and no father. What is her life going to be like?' She scrubbed the palm of her hand over her cheek and he frowned, helpless to know what to say.

'Angie seemed like a really nice girl and her mother was—'

'Angie is nothing more than a child, Jake!' She interrupted him, her voice fierce and her eyes glistening with more tears. 'A child! She should be playing with her friends, doing exams and dreaming about her future, instead of which she's going to be living the life of an adult. Do you have any idea what it's like, being a mother at the age of sixteen?' Her voice shook. 'Having a baby is daunting at any age but at sixteen it's nothing short of terrifying. So much responsibility when you're nothing more than a child yourself. And your whole life is suddenly violently rearranged. You can't do any of the things you should be doing. Instead of studying, you're changing nappies. Instead of going out with friends, you're pushing a pram. So you become isolated and lonely and no one really understands because all the teenagers you know are studying or partying and all the mothers you know are in their thirties, married with other children. No one is like you.' She broke off, her chest rising and falling, and he studied her face and wondered.

Even for an extremely tired, pregnant woman, her reaction was a little too emotional. 'We're not talking about Angie and Bonnie any more, are we?' He reached across the table and grabbed the box of tissues that was stacked on top of a pile of unopened post.

She took the tissue he offered her, blew her nose and then looked away. 'Ignore me—it's been a long and stressful night. I should probably go back to bed.' Her nose was blocked up, her dark lashes were damp from crying and he just wanted to cuddle her.

'You're never going to sleep in this state. You need to get it off your chest and then perhaps you'll be able to relax. Talk to me, Miranda. Tell me what's on your mind.' He hesitated and then decided to take a risk. 'I'm wondering why you care so much and I'm wondering why you know so much about it. Did it happen to you? Were you that mother you described so eloquently?'

'The mother?' She stared at the table and then at him. 'I wasn't the mother, Jake. I was the baby.'

His was silent for a moment, his eyes fixed on her pale face. 'You're—'

'My mother had me at sixteen. I was the baby.'

It made sense, of course. The reason she'd been so desperate to find Bonnie's mother. The way she'd understood Angie's situation. 'You were abandoned?'

Miranda reached for a tissue and blew her nose hard. 'I was luckier than Bonnie. My mother put me in a box covered in towels. Apparently I was in quite a good condition when I was found. She even wrote a note.'

Something twisted inside him but he fought the impulse to drag her into his arms. He knew that, right now, she needed to talk. 'And they traced your mother?'

She nodded. 'Oh, yes. It was all very embarrassing for my grandparents. Treasured only daughter suddenly going off the rails. They'd had such high hopes for her. She was top in her class and very pretty. The world was out there, just waiting for her to conquer it. Only she made a mistake and I came along.' She was silent for a moment, thoughtful. Then she gave a bright smile that was entirely false. 'But they did the right thing. They took me in and brought me up. I lived with them until my mum married Keith.'

'Was he your father?'

'No. Mum never said who my father was. Maybe she didn't know. Have you any idea how that feels?' She looked at him, her expression strangely blank. 'Sometimes I look in the mirror and I search for him. I think to myself, Are those his eyes? Do I have his mouth? Having no idea where you came from is a strange feeling.'

'But your mum did get married.'

'Oh, yes, she did very well for herself. Keith was a barrister. Great job. Public figure. Very well respected. On the outside, we looked like the perfect family.' The bitterness in her tone was unmistakable and Jake looked at her, a feeling of foreboding building inside him.

'And on the inside? Tell me about your stepfather.'

'I think he loved my mum. Or at least, his version of love.' She yanked another tissue out of the box and blew her nose again. 'Unfortunately he didn't feel the same way about me. I suppose I was a constant reminder of my mum's mistake. The one ugly blot on the otherwise perfect canvas of her life. Everything I did was wrong. He had a hideous temper.'

Jake felt his shoulders tense. 'How terrible. Are you saying he shouted at you? Or did he…?'

'Hit me? Was that what you wanted to ask?' She finished his unspoken question and gave a wan smile. 'Oh, yes. Often. But funnily enough that didn't upset me as much as his contempt. He so obviously couldn't stand the sight of me and that really, really hurt.'

'Didn't anyone know?'

'I didn't want to tell my friends, if that's what you mean. And none of them would have believed me anyway. They all thought I was so lucky.' She blew her nose again. 'Big house. Fancy holidays. Keith was capable of putting on a very impressive act when he had to but he was always so unpredictable I didn't dare take anyone home in case he lost his temper. So gradually I became isolated. They thought I was a snob who didn't want to mix with them. I didn't know how to make myself popular.' She twisted the tissue. 'And I suppose, if I'm honest, I didn't think I was very likeable. Keith had a way of making you feel pretty rotten about yourself.'

Jake let out a long breath and ran a hand over his face. The thought of how she must have suffered made his blood heat to dangerous levels. 'So that's why you were so appalled when I hit your landlord.'

She gave a wan smile. 'I suppose so. I'm not great with violence of any sort.'

Jake struggled to control his shock. She didn't need him to be shocked, she needed him to be supportive. 'Couldn't your mother do anything?'

'My mother didn't want to do anything to wreck her new-found respectability. She was moving in circles that she'd considered totally out of her reach. I mean, imagine it…' She suddenly sounded older than her years. 'She left school at sixteen, pregnant, and here she was, married to a rich barrister. Quite an achievement, and my mother was very achievement-focused. All she really cared about was how it looked to other people. Marrying Keith was a way of wiping out the mistakes of her past.'

'She condoned his behaviour?'

'She said he was a very busy man with a stressful job and I ought to try not to annoy him.'

Jake gritted his teeth. 'You didn't tell anyone else? Your teachers? Your GP?'

'My GP was his squash partner.' Miranda shook her head.

'No. I just tried not to annoy him. The trouble was, I annoyed him by just being me. So I learned to make myself as invisible as possible and I became very self-reliant.' She gave a tiny shrug. 'It's history now. Please, don't think I spend all day, every day thinking about it. It's over. It was over a long time ago and I refuse to be a victim.'

'But clearly you don't see them any more.'

She shook her head. 'I left home as soon as I could and they didn't try and stop me. It's affected me, of course it has. I suppose a psychologist would say that's why I got involved with Peter. Searching for a father figure.' She gave a smile of wry self-mockery. 'Ironic, really. In his own way he was about as good a father figure as Keith. In my head I've invented this mythical dad.'

'And what's he like?'

At first she looked surprised by the question and then she gave a little shrug. 'Ridiculously perfect. He adores his children so much that he's prepared to put them first and he actually enjoys spending time with them. He delights in their achievements and he wants to shield them from all harm.' She sat back in her chair, her expression shifting from tense to dreamy. 'And when I imagine him, he has this look in his eyes. Love, I suppose.' She sounded so wistful that Jake felt an ache building deep inside him. Obviously she'd never known the deep, unconditional love of a parent.

'So what would a psychologist say about your relationship with me?'

'We don't have a relationship.'

'No?' It gave him some satisfaction to see her drop the tissue. Her hand stilled.

'Jake, I—'

'I'm glad you told me because now I understand why you keep backing away. You don't believe that I'll be able to love your baby the way I love you. You don't believe I can love unconditionally.'

'You don't love me. Please, stop saying that.' She covered her face with her hands. 'You can't possibly love me.'

'Why not? Because your stepfather didn't love you? Because your mother didn't stand up for you? That doesn't make you unlovable, sweetheart, it just makes you unlucky. But luck can change and it's time yours did.'

Her hands dropped and she turned to look at him. 'Jake...'

Unable to help himself, he brought his mouth down on hers. Her lips, impossibly soft and sweet, parted under the insistent pressure of his. He felt the hot burn of arousal scorch his body but held himself back, not wanting to rush her, aware that she was still deeply upset and extremely vulnerable. If he'd stopped to think then he probably would have admitted to himself that it wasn't the best time to kiss her, but somehow thinking seemed impossible. He slid a hand into her silky hair and kept the kiss gentle and exploratory. He tasted hesitation and fear. Sensed her reluctance. And then she slid her arms round his neck and kissed him back, her tongue touching his.

The kiss was mindless, endless, and then she pulled back slightly, her dark eyes clouded.

'We shouldn't be doing this.'

He stroked a hand over the smoothness of her cheek. 'If you can give me one good reason why we should stop, I'll give it my full consideration.'

'I'm pregnant.'

'That's not a reason. You'll have to do better than that.' His lips brushed against hers and he felt her shiver of response.

'My New Year's resolution was to stop believing in romance.' Her voice was breathy and feminine and slid over his nerve endings, increasing his arousal several notches.

'New Year was weeks ago.' He nibbled at her lower lip. 'It's time you broke your resolution.'

'Jake…' She groaned his name against his mouth and he felt aching, tearing claws of lust drag through his loins. He couldn't remember feeling this desperate since he'd been a teenager and suddenly he felt his control slipping.

'Come upstairs with me, Miranda.' He stroked her hair away from her face and kissed her again. 'Now.'

'Yes.' She rose to her feet and he scooped her up into his arms, ignoring her soft gasp of surprise and protest.

'Put me down! You'll slip a disc or something. I weigh a ton.'

'You don't weigh anything,' Jake growled as he carried up the stairs to his bedroom. The curtains were open and moonlight shone through the windows, casting a gentle light over the room. 'You should be heavier than this. You definitely need to eat more. I'm going to devote tomorrow to feeding you.'

Her arms tightened around his neck as he laid her in the centre of the bed. 'What about tonight?'

'That's devoted to something else entirely.' He came down next to her and brought his mouth down on hers, forcing himself to take it slowly. Part of him wanted to strip her naked and take her fast but he knew that she deserved so much more than that. She deserved to be well and truly loved. So he kept his mouth gentle and his hands slow.

He felt her body shift under his, felt the urgency of her own response and removed her top in a smooth movement. Her breasts were perfectly rounded and he lowered his head with a groan of masculine appreciation.

'You're so beautiful.'

'I'm so fat.'

Even though he was aching and throbbing with need, her tiny plea for reassurance was so entirely feminine that it made him smile. 'Sweetheart—do I need to tell you how much I want you?'

She lifted a hand to his face and there was uncertainty in her eyes. 'Do you?'

'Can't you tell? I wanted you from the first moment I saw you sitting by that frozen lake. You looked at me and I was lost.' He moved his body so that she could be left in no doubt as to his own state of arousal and dragged the tips of his fingers over her nipple.

She arched towards him, her mouth damp from his kisses, her dark hair tumbled around her shoulders. She was all woman and her beauty drove all words from his head.

He didn't know how to tell her how he felt.

He only knew how to show her, so he lowered his head and his mouth touched first one breast, then the other. Then his tongue flickered out and he licked and teased before sucking her into the warmth of his mouth. He heard her soft gasp, felt her hands slide into his hair and grip.

He felt her body shift restlessly, felt the stroke of her leg against his, urging him on, but he discovered that he was no longer in a hurry. Who, in their right mind, would want to rush something so impossibly perfect?

He ignored her soft whimper and her searching hands and took his time, removing the rest of her clothes and his and then sliding his mouth down her silken skin, lingering on the curve of her abdomen before moving lower still to discover the heart of her.

He heard her faint gasp of protest turn to a moan of ecstasy as extended his voyage of discovery and pushed the boundaries of intimacy.

'Jake, please…' His name was a sob on her lips. 'Please…'

He knew what she wanted—*knew what she was asking for*—but he wanted more from her, wanted to push her to the very edge of sanity, and he used his fingers and mouth to do exactly that, his own arousal heightened by her cries and the fierce reaction of her body as he pushed her through clouds of sexual excitement to a powerful climax that rocked her whole body.

Only when the violent spasms finally ceased did he slide up the bed and roll onto his back. He was so aroused he thought he might explode, and he lay for a moment, trying to focus on something other than Miranda. Trying to regain some semblance of control.

And she was silent, too, eyes closed, her lashes dark against her pale cheeks.

'Miranda?' Worried about the lengthy silence, he turned his head towards her. 'Are you all right?'

'I'm not sure.' And then her eyes opened and she gave a slow, satisfied smile. Her gaze fixed on his, she slid a leg over him and then sat up, her cheeks flushed and her dark hair falling forward. 'Is it OK to do this?'

There was a purposeful, seductive gleam in her dark eyes that he found intensely arousing. Dimly aware that she'd asked him a serious question, Jake sucked in a breath and forced himself to think like an obstetrician. 'It's fine,' he groaned. 'I'll be gentle, I promise. Sweetheart, have I told you that you're incredible? And beautiful?'

Despite the intimacy of their position, her smile was shy. 'Do you need glasses?'

'No, I need *you*.' He slid his hands over her hips, positioned her carefully and felt the silken heat of her womanhood tease the tip of his arousal. Afraid that he might explode within seconds of entering her, he slowed the pace, controlling her movements, refusing to allow her the satisfaction she so clearly craved.

'Jake—I need to…' Her breathing shallow, she pushed his

hands away impatiently and sank onto him, taking him deep inside her, destroying his plans to take her gently and carefully.

Heat exploded through his sensitised body and he gave a harsh groan and opened his mouth to tell her to slow down, but she lowered her head and kissed him, her delicate tongue coaxing his into a dance every bit as intimate as the rest of their encounter.

Struggling to find his customary control, Jake tried to hold her hips but she grabbed his wrists and anchored them above his head, moving with a slow erotic rhythm that reduced his world to nothing but sensation.

Dimly he knew that this wasn't how he'd intended it to happen. He'd intended to orchestrate the whole thing but somehow she'd taken the initiative.

Reluctantly her mouth left his and she sat up, her hair sliding over her bare shoulders as she moved over him with the smooth grace of a dancer. The heat in his loins reached intolerable levels and he tried to warn her that she really, really needed to slow down, but the only sound that came from his mouth was a hoarse groan of encouragement. Aware of her own soft cry of release, he felt her body spasm around his and he exploded inside her with propulsive force, driven past the point at which he might have been able to regain his slippery hold on control.

She woke to find him watching her.

'Good morning.' His voice was husky and deep and he leaned forward to deliver a lingering kiss to her mouth. 'You slept well. I'm pleased. How are you feeling?'

Unsettled by the look in his eyes, she rolled onto her back. 'Fine.' Shy? Embarrassed? She thought of all the things she'd told him, *the things they'd done…*

'Fine? Miranda, do not, for one moment, think that you're going to be allowed to pretend that last night didn't happen.'

'I know it happened.' How could she not, when the memories were still so clear in her head?

'And do you also know that I love you?' He spoke softly and then raised himself up on one arm and looked down at her with a gentle smile. 'You're beautiful and good and I want you to be my wife. And, just in case you think I say those words to all the girls, you ought to know that I've never said that to anyone in my life before now.'

His wife?

Her stomach dropped and she looked into those sexy blue eyes and wished that her life wasn't filled with mountains to conquer. No matter how much she loved him, and she did love him, she'd never be able to say yes. She owed it to the baby to refuse him.

'No, Jake.'

'It isn't difficult, Miranda. All you have to do is say you love me, too, and I know you do.'

He was so confident, she thought enviously. Not arrogant, just very sure of himself.

'I care about you,' she said finally, her voice slow and still slightly husky from sleep. 'Of course I do. You've been an amazing friend to me, Jake.'

If she confessed that she loved him, there was no way he'd take no for an answer.

'Friend?' One dark brow lifted as he studied her face. 'Last night had absolutely nothing to do with friendship, Miranda.'

'Last night should never have happened. I was tired and emotional. I told you things that I've never shared with anyone and I probably shouldn't have said it to you but...' She tried to look away from him but he caught her chin in gentle fingers so that she was forced to look at him.

'Are you saying that I took advantage of you?'

'No.' She shook her head. 'I'm saying that I needed comfort and you—' She broke off and he sighed.

'Miranda, last night wasn't about comfort. Comfort was the box of tissues and the hug I gave you in the kitchen. Comfort was the hot chocolate that you didn't drink before you went to bed. What we shared last night had nothing whatsoever to do with comfort. It was hot sex and you know it.'

Memories heated her body and she closed her eyes tightly, trying to block it out and return to reality. *The reality of her life.* 'For goodness' sake, Jake—'

'Stop right there.' He put his fingers over her mouth. 'If this is this is the part where you remind me that you're pregnant, I don't want to hear it. I haven't forgotten that fact, angel. I love the fact that you're pregnant and I'm waiting for you to say that you'll marry me so that I can spend the next few weeks getting used to the idea of finally being a father. I'm aiming to be that ridiculously perfect dad that you've always dreamed about. I'm ready to adopt the baby as my own. I'm ready to love it as my own, if you'll let me.'

Miranda lay there, staring temptation in the face. She loved him, she knew that without a doubt. She loved him for the man he was. But nothing changed the fact that she was having another man's child.

And she, better than anyone, understood the implications of that.

'It would always come between us,' she whispered, 'if not now, then later. He or she might be naughty and you'd be fed up.'

His mouth tightened and she saw a flash of anger in his eyes. 'Let's get one thing straight right now—I'm not your stepfather and I never will be. Neither am I the man who fathered your baby, which I'm actually glad about because he doesn't sound like much of a human being. I love you, Miranda, and I love the baby, too, because it's part of you. And that love is unconditional. Family life isn't always smooth and doesn't come with guarantees, I know that. And all children are naughty sometimes, that's what childhood is all about. And I'm sure that sometimes I *will* get fed up because I'm human just like you, but I'm never going to regret being a father to the baby, I'm not going to bail out, if that's what worries you, and I'm not going to hit anyone. Unless someone threatens a member of my family, that isn't my style.'

She knew from the dangerous gleam in his eyes that he was thinking about her landlord and something shifted inside her. *He'd defended her.*

'I know it seems simple to you, but I can't risk it, Jake.' She squeezed her eyes tightly shut, unable to watch the pain in his eyes. She told herself that she was doing them both a favour. She was saving three people from greater hurt. 'We should never have done what we did last night because now our relationship is awkward. I'll move out. I should have found somewhere long ago but it was so comfortable here and…' And she'd loved being with Jake. She left the words unspoken and rose out of bed, determined to make it to the bathroom before she made a fool of herself.

She seemed to spend her entire life crying at the moment, she reflected as she bolted the door behind her and sank down onto the edge of the bath.

She was doing the right thing, she knew she was.

But if she was doing the right thing, why did it feel so hard?

CHAPTER TEN

OVER the next week or two, the weather grew colder still and Miranda found it impossible to feel anything but tired and miserable.

She thought she'd be relieved to give up work but once she did she found that she missed the friendship of her colleagues on the labour ward. She felt as though she'd made lifetime friends. For the first time in her life she felt as though she was home.

But home was becoming a touchy subject.

She couldn't carry on living with Jake so she'd been desperately scouring the local paper for flats. She'd found one that would have been all right, but the landlord had said that it wasn't available until the spring and she couldn't wait that long. She needed somewhere now.

At this rate she was going to be living with Jake when the baby arrived, she thought as she trawled through the paper once again for possibilities.

Not that he made things awkward. On the contrary, he was extremely kind to her but somehow that just made it worse.

She was drinking coffee and summoning up the energy to go and see a small flat a mile away from Jake's house when there was a knock on the door.

She opened it to find Christy standing there with a basket in her hand.

'I'm playing Little Red Riding Hood,' she said cheerfully, handing Miranda the basket and walking past her into the house. 'I was baking with my daughter Katy this morning and we thought you might like some. I remember what it was like when I was almost due. I was starving hungry but I couldn't summon up the energy to cook anything. There's bread, scones, some cheese from the deli and some chutney we made last summer from the apples in our garden.'

Miranda carried the basket through to the kitchen. 'That's really kind of you.'

'Not that kind.' Christy shrugged off her coat and dropped it over the chair. 'I actually had an ulterior motive for coming here. Can I put the kettle on?'

'Help yourself.' Miranda put the basket on the table and looked at her warily. 'What's your ulterior motive?'

For a moment Christy didn't answer and her back was towards Miranda so it was impossible to read her face. She filled the kettle and then she turned. 'I'm worried about Jake.'

'You're worried about him?' Miranda felt a vicious stab of fear. 'Why? What's happened?'

Christy frowned. '*You've* happened. He's in love with you and I gather it isn't reciprocated. He's thoroughly miserable. Crotchety and short-tempered, thoroughly unlike our easygoing Jake. '

Miranda bit her lip. 'I know he thinks he's in love with me, but—'

'If you're suggesting that Jake doesn't know his own mind, maybe you don't understand him as well as you think you do. I could help you out there.' Christy dipped her hand into the basket and helped herself to one of her own scones. 'Jake knows exactly what he wants in life and he's never wrong. He doesn't change his mind about things. He knew almost from day one that he wanted to be an obstetrician and he was right. It's the perfect specialty for him. And it's the same with women. He doesn't fall in love easily.'

'He was in love with you.'

'Yes.' Christy's voice was calm as she split the scone with a knife and spread each half with butter. 'I think he was, for a short while. And that's one of the biggest compliments I've ever been paid because Jake doesn't fall in love easily so when he does, it's a really big thing. And he's in love with you.'

'Maybe he is.' Miranda sat down on the nearest chair. 'But I'm having another man's baby.'

'I know about that.' Christy put half the scone on a plate and pushed it towards her. 'Eat. Jake's worried that you're not eating enough so I said I'd take charge of your calorie intake between now and delivery.'

Miranda smiled. 'No one has ever fussed over me before the way he does.'

'No?' Christy's eyes were gentle. 'Then make the most of it. Grab it while you can. He wants the baby, Miranda. He wants the baby as much as he wants you, can't you believe that?'

'I believe that he thinks that's the case.' Miranda stared at the scone on her plate. 'But people don't know how they're going to react. The baby isn't his. Nothing can ever change that.'

'And he doesn't want to. Jake is the most balanced, level-headed guy you could ever hope to meet. Have you ever seen him panic?'

'No. No I haven't. He's always Mr Super Cool.'

Christy nodded. 'He's a guy who knows who he is and knows what he wants. And he wants you and the baby. Think about it. Think about what you might be turning down.'

'What if, two years from now, he's tired of having a lively toddler around the house?'

Christy looked at her for a long moment and then stood up, a sad smile on her face. 'If you have to ask me that question, you obviously don't know Jake at all,' she said softly as she picked up her coat. 'He's a good man. A hell of a catch, frankly. You should remember that. Of all the women he's ever dated, you're the one he wants. Wow. Be flattered. And now I need to get going because it's snowing again and Alessandro worries about me when the roads are bad. Don't get up. You look tired. Eat your scone and I'll see myself out.'

Miranda sat in the kitchen, staring out of the window as the snow fell and darkness closed in. Jake had phoned earlier to say that he was going down to A and E to deal with an emergency and he was likely to be very late. And she missed him. Even in such a short time she'd become used to the life they'd led. She'd enjoyed their routine of working together and living together. Now it was just the living and soon it wouldn't even be that because she intended to move into a new flat in the next two weeks.

Outside the wind whistled around the house and she couldn't stop thinking about everything that Christy had said about Jake. Phrases kept running through her head.

'*A hell of a catch.*'

'*You're the one he wants.*'

And he was the one she wanted, too.

And suddenly she knew that Christy was right. Jake was nothing like her father and nothing like Peter. He was strong and sexy, kind and tough, all at the same time. And she was crazy about him.

And Christy was right—he did know what he wanted out of life.

And he wanted her and the baby, so why was she turning

down the chance of happiness when she was madly in love with him? When she knew he'd make a wonderful partner?

A slow warmth spread through her and she smiled. She was going to talk to him. As soon as he came home from work. She was going to tell him that she'd changed her mind. That she wanted him to adopt the baby. *That she wanted them to be a family.*

Wanting to look her best, she washed and dried her hair, changed into a loose, comfortable dress and made herself a drink.

But there was still no sign of Jake. And she was desperate to talk to him. Suddenly it seemed imperative that he know how she felt.

Feeling jumpy and restless, she stood up and paced around the kitchen and then moved into the living room. She was standing there, staring at the photograph of Jake rolling in the snow with his two nephews, when the first pain hit her.

She gave a cry of shock and clutched at her abdomen, winded by the pain and unable to move. Gradually it eased and she inched her way towards the sofa, trying to talk rationally to herself.

She wasn't due for another month. These were just more Braxton-Hicks' contractions, signs that her body was preparing for labour. She'd felt them before, although never with such severity. The pain would fade and then everything would be fine.

It took less than two minutes for her to realise that everything was far from fine. Less than two minutes for another pain to tear through her body, this time so severe that she was unable to breathe or cry out. She dropped to her knees, closed her eyes and forced herself not to panic.

She was fairly sure that she was in labour.

Fairly sure?

If she hadn't been so frightened, she would have laughed.

She was a midwife, for goodness' sake. And she didn't even know whether she was in labour.

Phone.

She needed to get to the phone.

Trying to be calm and rational, she waited for the pain to fade and then staggered over to Jake's phone, only to discover that the line was dead.

Realising that she was going to have to do this on her own, she grabbed some cushions from the sofa and settled herself on the floor to await the next pain.

It would be all right, she told herself, rubbing a hand over her stomach and feeling the tightening against her hand. This time when the pain came she was ready for it and she closed her eyes and breathed the way she'd taught countless pregnant women to breathe in the antenatal classes she'd run.

The pain thundered through her, relentless in its intensity, and she suddenly knew why women were encouraged to have someone with them when they gave birth. You needed someone on the outside. You needed someone who was one step removed from what was happening. You needed love and support—

'Miranda?'

Her eyes flew open and she saw Jake standing in the doorway. His dark hair was dusted with snow and a long coat emphasised his powerful physique. A rush of cold air blew into the room before he closed the door firmly.

'Labour…' she gasped, and then closed her eyes and tried to concentrate on her breathing as another pain hit.

'How far apart?' He was on his knees beside her, his hands freezing as they slid over her abdomen, feeling the contraction. 'When did it start?'

She had to wait for the pain to fade before she could speak. 'Not long ago. And hardly any time apart. I think it's coming, Jake. I know it's a month early, but I'm definitely in labour.'

'You should have called me.'

'Phone not working.' She closed her eyes as she felt another pain hit and then swell to almost unbearable levels before fading back again. But this time she wasn't on her own. This time she felt a strong arm round her shoulders as Jake held her and praised her.

The moment the pain had passed he reached for the phone and then cursed softly and slammed it down again. 'The line must be dead and I've got no signal on my mobile.'

She looked at him with fear in her eyes. 'Jake…'

'Don't worry about it.' He shrugged his broad shoulders out of his coat. 'How do you feel about a home birth?'

'Nervous?'

'That's not very flattering.' He teased her as he stripped off his jumper and pushed up his sleeves. 'I'm an obstetrician. This is my territory.'

'No, it isn't.' She closed her eyes and shifted her position, ready for the next pain. 'You deal with complications. This is supposed to be a normal birth. You obstetricians don't know anything about normal births.'

'Well, I'm sure I'll struggle through and if it all seems a bit bewilderingly normal, I'll just have to turn it round and deliver it as a breech.'

Despite the pain, she managed a laugh. 'You're mad, do you know that?'

'Relax, Miranda. Everything is going to be fine.' He stroked her hair away from her face with a gentle hand and then switched into consultant mode. 'Another contraction?' He took her hand and eased her into a better position, talking to her gently until the wave of pain receded. Then he tried both phones again and shook his head. 'Nothing. Miranda, I think I'd better examine you. I need to know how many centimetres dilated you are. If this baby is about to arrive, I need to boil kettles and do all the other useless and pointless things they do in the movies.'

It was impossible to panic in the face of his humour and confidence.

'You can't examine me, it's too embarrassing. Oh, Jake…' She screwed up her face and sobbed with pain. 'Is it supposed to feel like this? It's agony.' Another pain hit and she was hit by a wave of nausea. 'I feel sick…'

He reached for a decorative ceramic bowl and placed it in front of her. 'Don't worry about it, just keep breathing.' His voice was calm and steady. 'Miranda, I think you're in transition.'

He was behaving like a cool professional while all she wanted was for him to hug her and tell her that he loved her. But she'd sent him away, hadn't she? She'd told him that she didn't want him in her life.

She grabbed his hand and closed her eyes. 'I'm scared—' She broke off as another pain hit her and he waited for it to pass and then gently disengaged himself and stood up.

'Where are you going?' There was a distinct note of panic in her voice and he gave her a reassuring smile.

'For some reason unknown to me, I have a sterile cord clamp in my car so I'm going to fetch that and then I'm going to wash my hands. I think I'm about to deliver a baby.'

She closed her eyes with a groan of denial. 'I can't believe this is happening.' Then she gave a gasp. 'Jake! I want to push. Oh—I can feel the head.'

'Don't push until I've washed my hands.' He strode out of the room but was back moments later with an armful of towels and sheets.

'I *can* feel the head, Jake.' She grabbed his hand again, 'I'm scared.'

'There's nothing to be scared about. Miranda, I just need to take a look and see what's happening.' His voice was gentle and calm and suddenly she wasn't embarrassed any more, she was just worried.

It wasn't supposed to be like this.

'It's far too quick! Don't let anything happen to the baby. What if the cord is round the neck? What if there's something wrong with the foetal heart and we don't even know because I'm not on a monitor?' The words came out in a rush and she broke off as another pain hit and the desire to push was so intense that she could do nothing except follow the instructions of her body.

'The head's coming now, Miranda. Stop pushing. Stop pushing, angel. Pant, that's right... Good girl. Everything's fine.'

She closed her eyes tightly and tried to get her breath back but then another pain swamped her and her body pushed the baby out and into Jake's waiting arms. The baby howled angrily and Miranda sat back with a rush of relief.

'Is the baby all right?' She felt completely shocked by the speed and violence of it all. If Jake hadn't been there, she didn't know what she would have done.

'Not a baby. A little girl, and she seems absolutely fine.' Jake's voice was strangely flat. 'She's beautiful. Well done.'

He placed the baby carefully in her arms and she stared down at the tiny, perfect features with wonder in her eyes. The howls turned to whimpers as the baby nuzzled Miranda's breast.

'Good idea.' Brisk and businesslike, Jake settled himself into a more comfortable position. 'Feed her, Miranda, if you can. I don't have any drugs with me. Nothing to help your uterus contract so we're going to have to do this the way that nature intended as well. Physiological third stage. Feed her. It will help your uterus contract.'

Some women opted to have a physiological third stage, but Miranda knew that the risks of bleeding were greater and understood why Jake was now paying her more attention than ever. He was worried that she might bleed and he had no access to a telephone.

He was a doctor doing his job.

And he didn't seem at all interested in the baby.

She undid the buttons of her maternity dress and gently lifted the baby to her breast. With remarkably little encouragement, the baby latched onto her nipple and sucked happily. Miranda breathed a sigh of relief but suddenly the happiness of the birth mingled with despair. She wanted to say something, want to speak, but none of the words in her head felt right.

Seemingly oblivious to her emotional state, Jake slid a hand over her abdomen, checking her uterus. 'Everything feels fine.'

And everything was fine. The placenta came away easily and Jake breathed a sigh of relief.

'I don't know what you midwives complain about.' He dragged a forearm over his forehead and gave a lopsided smile. 'Piece of cake. I'm just going to wash my hands and find another heater to put in here. This room isn't warm enough for her.'

He vanished for a moment and the returned with two heaters, a drink for Miranda and the phone in his hand.

'The phone's working again. I want you to go into hospital, Miranda. She looks fine to me and you look fine, too, but it was all a bit quick for my liking and the roads are so bad that we wouldn't be able to get you to hospital in a hurry if it suddenly became necessary.'

Miranda frowned. 'Do I have to?'

'Just for tonight. Oh, by the way, there was a message on the machine. Someone about a flat. The landlord told you it wasn't available until the spring but apparently the tenants have found somewhere else and are moving today, so it's yours whenever you want it.'

She waited for him to say something about not wanting her to leave but he said nothing at all, just finished clearing up, fetched her a few things that he knew she'd need and made a few notes to give to the ambulance crew.

And he still didn't look at the baby.

Which meant only one thing as far as she was concerned. He wasn't interested in her, Miranda thought miserably, holding back the tears that threatened.

It was late the following afternoon when Jake walked up to the side room. In his arms were a teddy bear and a huge bunch of flowers.

This, he decided as he put a hand on the door and steeled himself to open it, was going to be one of the hardest five minutes of his life.

He was going to deliver the flowers, say all the things he was expected to say and then just get out as fast as he could, hopefully before he made a complete and utter fool of himself.

Taking a deep breath, he pushed open the door and walked into the room, a smile pinned on his face. The smile faded instantly when he saw that the room was empty.

And then he heard a faint gurgle coming from the cot by the bed and he realised that the room wasn't empty at all. The baby was in the cot. But there was no sign of Miranda.

Wondering why he was intent on torturing himself, he stepped over to the cot and stared down.

The baby lay with her eyes closed, her tiny mouth moving in her sleep.

Jake felt his heart twist. 'Hi, there.' His voice was soft as he reached down and touched her cheek. 'It's nice to meet you properly.'

* * *

Miranda paused in the doorway of her bathroom, her eyes on Jake.

He obviously didn't realise she was in the room and he was talking to the baby. *Touching her.*

'I didn't get a good look at you yesterday,' he was saying softly, a gentle look in his eyes as he leaned over the cot. 'I was too busy worrying about your mum.'

Miranda frowned. He'd been worried about her? He certainly hadn't seemed worried.

The baby gurgled sleepily and Jake smiled. 'You're going to make your mum very happy. Which is a good thing, because it's what she deserves.'

'Jake?' Miranda stepped into the room and he turned to face her, his eyes suddenly wary.

'I didn't know you were there.'

'I was using the bathroom.' She looked at him. 'I—I heard what you said. I didn't know you were worried about me.'

He gave a faint smile. 'You were eavesdropping on a private conversation.'

'Why were you worried? You're a brilliant obstetrician and I've never known you worry about anyone before.'

He stared at her for a long moment and then he gave a humourless laugh. 'I've never been called on to deliver the baby of the woman I love before. Believe me, it's entirely different. Objectivity flies out of the window. I was scared to death.'

Her heart fluttered in her chest. 'The woman you love?'

He shook his head and gave a weary smile. 'I can't argue this with you again, Miranda.' He handed her the flowers and put the teddy bear down on the bed. 'These are for you. I know you'll be coming home later, but everyone needs flowers when they're in hospital. And now I ought to go. I have a clinic and—'

'The clinic can wait.' She clutched the flowers against her chest, her breathing unsteady. 'You haven't told me that you love me since that night we made love. And yesterday, when the baby was born, you hardly looked at her. I assumed that I'd ruined everything. That you'd changed your mind. About her and about me.'

He was silent for a moment and then he ran a hand over the back of his neck, visibly tense. 'Does it really make any difference how I feel, Miranda?'

'Actually, yes, it does.' Her voice cracked and she found herself hoping that the baby wouldn't wake up for a few minutes. There were things that she needed to say, things that were so difficult for her she couldn't risk being interrupted.

But Jake spoke first. 'All right. I wasn't going to say this now. Giving birth is an emotional time for a woman and I wanted to give you some space, but I may as well be honest. You're right when you said that I didn't look at the baby. I didn't. And the reason for that was that I didn't dare. I knew that if I looked at her, all attempts at being one step removed and functioning as an obstetrician would fly out of the window. You gave birth very quickly, Miranda.' His tone was quiet and serious. 'No end of things could have gone wrong and I wanted to make sure that they didn't. I couldn't afford the distraction.'

'And that's why you seemed so detached? Uninterested?'

He walked across to the window and stared out across the hospital car park. 'I wasn't uninterested.'

'What then?'

'It was self-protection.' He turned. 'Because if I'd looked at the baby then I would have fallen in love with her and I can't afford to do that. It's bad enough losing you, without losing her as well.'

'Losing me?'

'You're moving out and you're taking the baby with you. And I don't know how to stop you. I don't know how to prove to you that I love you and I don't know how to prove to you that I love your daughter.'

'I thought it was too late. I thought you'd changed your mind.' Miranda closed her eyes and allowed the happiness to flood through her. 'All night I lay awake, fantasising about you saying those words.'

He frowned. 'Why would you have to fantasise when you knew how I felt?'

'Because I thought you'd changed your mind. You were so cool and detached when you delivered her, I thought that reality had finally hit home. It seemed as though you couldn't wait to get the pair of us out of your house and into hospital.'

'In a way I couldn't,' he confessed. 'I didn't want to put more pressure on you at that particular moment when all your attention should have been on your new baby. And you'd already made it clear how you felt.'

'No.' She shook her head. 'That isn't true. I told you about my fears. I told myself that I had to protect the baby at all costs. What I didn't tell you was that I love you, too. I knew it weeks ago, but I knew if I admitted it you'd never take no for an answer.'

He stilled. 'But if you loved me, why would you want me to take no for an answer?'

'Because I have a responsibility towards my daughter. I'm responsible for her happiness. I thought that promise meant never marrying anyone.' She put the flowers down carefully. 'But then I realised that my daughter's happiness might involve giving her an amazing father. You. I was ready to tell you last night but then I went into labour.'

For a moment he just stood there, staring at her, and then he muttered something under his breath, crossed the room and hauled her into his arms.

'I can't believe you're saying those words,' he groaned against her neck. 'I've been planning my next move with the precision of a military campaign. I've been planning ways to persuade you to trust me enough to marry me.'

'You don't need a military campaign. I trust you, Jake.' She slid her arms round his neck. 'I love you.'

'And I love you.' He lowered his mouth to hers and kissed her long and hard. Then he lifted his head and stroked her hair away from her face. 'How could you possibly think my feelings had changed?'

'I pushed you away—I assumed you'd given up.'

He gave a slow smile. 'I don't give up easily, sweetheart. You should know that about me by now.' He studied her face for a long moment and his smile faded. 'It's important that you understand that. No matter what happens, nothing is going to stop me loving you and the baby. Nothing.'

'You've no idea how it feels to hear you say that.'

'Well, you'd better get used to it because I'm going to be saying it all the time. And what about you?' He hugged her closer. 'As a matter of interest, what changed your mind?'

'I didn't exactly change my mind. I knew I loved you. The only thing that changed was that I decided to tell you. Last night Christy came to see me and after she left I sat in the dark and did a lot of thinking.'

He gave a short laugh. 'That explains the mess in my kitchen. I wondered where the scones came from.'

'She told me a few things. Things that I already knew. Things I was allowing myself to ignore because of Keith.'

'What things?'

'That you're a good man. That you were fully aware of the responsibility you'd be taking on, that if you said you wanted the baby, too, you meant it…'

He frowned and his gaze turned to the cot where the baby

lay sleeping. 'It doesn't feel like a responsibility, Miranda. It feels like a gift.'

At that moment the baby woke up and started to whimper. Miranda smiled at Jake. 'Go on, then—if you're going to be her father, you'd better start getting to know her.'

'Have you thought of a name? I can't keep calling her "the baby".'

Miranda brushed her hair out of her eyes. 'Can we call her Hope?'

'Hope Blackwell.' Jake said it slowly and then nodded. 'Hope. Sounds good. What made you think of it?'

She hesitated. 'It's what you've given me. When we met on Christmas Day I was in the depths of despair. I was cold, lost and completely alone,' she said softly, 'and then you appeared out of the mist. And from then on, no matter how many times I tried to push you away, you were always by my side. And that made everything better. I'd grown up believing that happy families were an illusion, but you've convinced me that I'm wrong.'

He smiled and lifted the baby out of the cot. 'So are you giving me Hope or am I giving you Hope?'

'Both.' She watched him. Watched the tender way he held the baby. How could she have doubted him? Feeling ridiculously happy, she sat down in the chair and prepared to feed the baby. 'I'd better ring that man and tell him I no longer want the flat.'

'No need.' Jake placed the baby carefully in her arms. 'I've already done it.'

'You have?' Her eyes widened. 'Why?'

'Because there was no way I was letting you move out! I was buying myself more time.'

She shook her head in amazement. 'You're manipulative, do you know that? Some might even call you arrogant.'

'The word is constant.' He leaned forward and kissed her. 'I'm in love, Miranda. And seeing the baby just doubled my determination to marry you. Two for the price of one. My girls. I love you.'

'And I love you, too.'

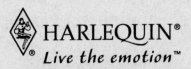

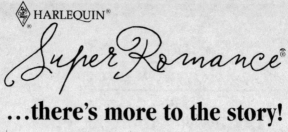

...there's more to the story!

Superromance.
A *big* satisfying read about unforgettable
characters. Each month we offer *six* very different
stories that range from family drama to adventure
and mystery, from highly emotional stories to
romantic comedies—and much more! Stories
about people you'll believe in and care about.
Stories too compelling to put down....

Our authors are among today's *best* romance
writers. You'll find familiar names and talented
newcomers. Many of them are award winners—
and you'll see why!

If you want the biggest and best
in romance fiction, you'll get it
from Superromance!

Exciting, Emotional, Unexpected...

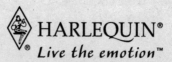

Harlequin® Historical
Historical Romantic Adventure!

*Imagine a time of chivalrous
knights and unconventional ladies,
roguish rakes and impetuous
heiresses, rugged cowboys
and spirited frontierswomen——
these rich and vivid tales will
capture your imagination!*

*Harlequin Historical . . .
they're too good to miss!*

HARLEQUIN®
INTRIGUE®

BREATHTAKING ROMANTIC SUSPENSE

Shared dangers and passions lead to electrifying
romance and heart-stopping suspense!

Every month, you'll meet six new heroes
who are guaranteed to make your spine tingle
and your pulse pound. With them you'll enter
into the exciting world of Harlequin Intrigue—
where your life is on the line
and so is your heart!

THAT'S INTRIGUE—
ROMANTIC SUSPENSE
AT ITS BEST!

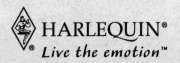

HARLEQUIN®
Live the emotion™